*To those of us who get up every day to see reality
crumbling into nothing:
I see you. I feel you. Despair, as I do.
Then find those you hold dear, and revel in the strength of
that connection.
Be stronger for it.*

May Day Flowers
By Faeri Sami

*To be truly radical is to make hope possible
rather than despair convincing.*

— Raymond Williams

# Table of Contents



Looking for something to listen to?

~ May Day Flowers Playlist ~

# Content Warnings

This novel contains the following:

- Mention of emotional and physical abuse by family (in the past) and related trauma episodes;
- Maladaptive daydreaming episodes;
- Loss of loved ones by illness (in the past);
- (Temporary) loss of limbs;
- Fire related wounds.

It also contains explicit sex scenes with:

- Body worship;
- Edging;
- Anal play;
- Vine bondage and play;
- Toy play;
- Role reversal;
- Minor shapeshifting.

All explicit scenes are marked by the <u>underlining</u> of the chapter's title where it happens; moreover, as things start to get steamy, you will see the folliage in the background of this page appear as a divider.

Feel free to skip them if you wish to. Please be kind to yourself, and happy reading!

# Chapter 1

When a tree hibernates, deep in the forest — if there is no one to listen to it…
Is it truly dreaming?

Far away from the hustle and bustle of downtown, through a beaten dirt path lined with thick, ancient flora, a house lies. In the middle of this building, fortressed by the dark stone walls in a vast central patio, a birch tree rests. Still mostly bare from the winter, it sits bigger and taller than any other birch in these woods — a soft constant hum accompanying, almost a breath, emanating from its core.

In. Out. In.

Ancient. Magical.

From a point where branches and trunk meet, a bundle of fresh leaves sways with the chilly breeze of the imminent twilight. Back and forth, side to side, they dance, shake, grow. The movement builds, bigger and bigger until it erupts in a flowery shower of particles, settling in a drape across a figure that takes its place.

Made of the same material of its rebirth — white bark speckled with darker stripes, languid extremities come to a rest as they sit down, breathing heavily. Their hair is nothing more than vines upon vines of auburn, ochre and moss, as long as their body, curling at the tips. Naked, bare as the tree that sprouted them once more this year, they shiver

and look up to the fading sky. Shaky words leave their lips with cost, and they bring a hand to their chest. Calm.

"I'm— alive— again…"

But, unexpectedly, this is not uttered in joy or, much less, reverence. Inside, the turmoil of leaves labours still. The figure coils, bringing their mind and heart to the tree that holds them below in a surprisingly human gesture. For figure and prop are one and the same — body and spirit, respectively. Yet they lie there, waiting for an answer from the heart, any answer. But it does not change.

In. Out. Now, their own, in this much more fragile body.

Ainsley has been their most recent of names — given to them by the last family to visit before saying goodbye again. Their last goodbye. They cannot remember how long it has been since then, but they do vividly recall past periods of earth-walking. Living by themselves in this place, roaming the forest for days on end, adventuring in the city nearby only to feel even more lost in the maze of signed streets; even lonelier in the waves of people passing by. Rinse, repeat, until winters come as it will and resets the cycle anew.

Again.

They catch another shiver and decide it would be better to ruminate in some warm clothes by the kitchen's fire.

Being so removed from society, most would think of it as a summer retreat, so close to the natural beauties of the highlands — lochs, cairns, miles and miles of oaks and braes. A mansion worthy of a long line of nobles, to be filled with life for a few weeks a year and then left abandoned for the rest of it. Surely, that is what it is.

But to some now residing closer to the city, and even fewer town hall officials, the history of this place is completely different. For they know that this building, on paper, was created in a single individual's name how-many-years ago, and has never since left it. And truly, in heart, it has never belonged to anyone in particular but instead freely given home to a particular kind of person. The kind to need long runs in the woods on a full moon, to those that must live close to a body of water, or perhaps to the kind of soul that cannot thrive amongst a crowd.

Once, this mansion sheltered and protected many a family of such kind, a constant hearth in a world that persecuted them. But when man created Industry (and with it, a new power system), as it made its way north and spread everywhere, well… Some felt persuaded, if not obliged to uproot their lives and try their luck amidst those that once shunned them, hiding their differences in plain sight.

One by one, for varying reasons, they would leave. One by one, the rooms would empty, the days would quiet, and the winters elongate until a single soul was left. Regrettably, someone that could not physically detach themself from this local, the titular 'owner' of a mansion for none.

They find themself taking fabric dust covers off most furniture before rummaging for a nice pair of linen, wide-brimmed trousers and a tightly-knit cardigan to go over a button-up shirt. Most of the rooms of this house have been locked for decades now — Ainsley only really uses a single bedroom upstairs. A simple, spacious area with only a double bed in plain sheets, an old fireplace opposite of it, a wardrobe to the side and double doors that open directly to the patio below by an arched balcony.

Finding most of their shoes eaten away by some long-gone critter, they decide to forgo footwear and do something about their much-too-long vines. A quick trim and some loose braiding behind them later, Ainsley takes a long look in their wardrobe's mirror and finds themselves in a 'she' kind of mood.

And so it is, at least for now.

Finally content with her form, she heads down to the kitchen and for a moment completely ignores the boiler, making a beeline for the only fireplace that hasn't been shut down — just in case. But before she has a chance to procure some kindling and wood, Ainsley hesitates.

Surely, no one would have cared to keep the heat system in check. She doesn't know exactly the number of years she has been in slumber this time around, but to hope for the pipes to be in order, the electricity to still be running, this far out...

Yet she finds herself by the boiler. A button press here, one there, and suddenly it comes to life with a loud hum, enacting a loud yelp from her, one that echoes in the room.

And then, laughter. Both in reaction to the startled situation she finds herself in, but also in the simple joy of being wrong.

It's funny — she roams the first floor and finds the lights working, the telephone line on, the television humming with static; and on the dining table in the kitchen, under a clear skylight dome, correspondence. Some of it, yes, just worthless ads that will spend more time in the bin than her hands. But two letters catch her eyes immediately.

One almost looks like junk mail, but the return address catches Ainsley's attention:

*"Hilltop Real Estate, Limited."*

She doesn't dare open it, knowing exactly what kind of message she will find attached inside. It might be written in kind, it might be aggressive, or even passive. But this is not the first time someone has tried to buy this land. And truthfully she couldn't care less about papers and names and laws — Ainsley doesn't own the land, she *is* the land.

She couldn't care less if some of these individuals just wanted to live among these trees, tend to the land. She would gladly welcome them with open arms, help them build the house of their dreams, keep them company. But it was never that, was it?

An amusement park, a factory, a train station — so many projects, so many ideas. Yet she could see right through their promises of advancement and betterment.

Money.

But of course, none of these people care about the consequences to the land, to Ainsley. Which just means they keep coming back, no matter what she does. Or, worse yet, they keep sending people who do give their time to listen to her but are forced to be there with an offer, for one reason or another.

Usually, money — again. But those individuals she understands better, and they understand her too.

Let them come, it doesn't matter. She will do what she always does. She will hold on. Let them face her in person, at least.

Ainsley throws that letter in the bin without a second thought.

The second letter is much more interesting, however. She recognises the name instantly: Estelle Lorelei-Waris.

The hyphenated surname surprises her, she admits, but she could not misplace that handwriting even if she wanted to. Estelle, last she saw her, was a young woman of barely nineteen summers, of strong opinions and even stronger temperament. She lived together with her coven in a house not too far from there, maybe a half-an-hour if you knew your way.

Which Ainsley does, of course. In her last earth-walk, Estelle and she became good friends — mostly because Estelle was in constant fight with her coven's policies, so she would often flee to Ainsley for a listening ear and a cup of jasmine tea. Ainsley would gladly lend a crying shoulder and would always be the diplomatic voice trying to keep the peace between coven and Estelle together. It worked, most of the time.

She wonders what came of her, and wastes no time opening her letter.

*'Ainsley, darling, I hope you had a good rest.*

*It's May of 2024 as I write this to you. I don't know if you'll be waking up this year, or if you'll even find this letter, but just in case you do… Come over for some chatting over lunch, yeah? We have a lot to catch up on. If I'm not in, here's my number (phones are mobile now, you'll reach me).'*

Mobile, huh? Ainsley looks over to her static device on the wall — a faded white, rotating numbers and coil cord, a small notebook and pencil resting on top. She indents the paper, dragging a finger over the number given to her, but decides she needs to see how the world has changed in all those years of sleep with her own eyes.

A chat over a meal sounds delightful.

So, still barefoot, she affords herself a leather side bag and a thicker coat over her for the trek, and into the forest she goes.

❧

A half-an-hour walk Ainsley expected, and half-an-hour it took. She finds herself much more centred after roaming through the trees and bushes of her backyard. May, Estelle wrote, but Ainsley did not need more information than a year date.

Everywhere she looks, the forest sings and blooms. There's a good quantity of mushrooms still lingering from winter, but the wild berries and budding fruit trees emanate a distinct sweet smell in the air that permeates the entire evening — some species, perhaps, a bit earlier than expected. But she does not linger.

By the time she reaches the end of her hike, just by the cairn's foot, her once empty bag is filled with dandelions, wild garlic, hawthorn and a handful of velvet shank caps. She even gave some of her forage to a passing wild rabbit family — and still, she had more than enough for a nice meal or two.

As she crosses the bend of the hill, the coven house emerges in her vision. Its gothic architecture is unchanged, and its imposing tower by the back of the state stands tall against the strong winds. The atmosphere, however, could not be more different.

Laughter, children's laughter reaches her first, intermingled with a distinct howl. Young as well, but if memory does not fail her, it sounds nothing like a creature of the forest — not wild enough.

*Werewolf.*

Must be. Suddenly the new surname inscribed on that letter falls into place.

Ainsley reaches the tall iron gates of the estate and is surprised to find a young tween leaning against the fence as she crosses the threshold. An eerily familiar face greets her, if not softer, their gaze disinterestedly locking with hers, arms crossed.

A moment passes in awkward silence before Ainsley breaks it.

"…Estelle?"

"Ainsley!" The voice comes instead from inside, as the actual Estelle stops by her porch.

Now over a decade older, her smile carries permanent marks on her face, adding to her powerful presence. Even in weather like this, her deep V-neck and perfectly ironed slacks complement her shaggy umber hair as it gets tussled on her run to meet Ainsley.

They meet halfway in a tight hug, swaying, making up for lost time.

"Darling, you're back! I can't believe my eyes. Thank all the stars. You look so different too!" Estelle breaks the hug to give Ainsley the space for a quick twirl.

"Yes, it seems womanhood has called me this time. Although I've given it my own touch."

"And it suits you. I have to ask, though — What's with the shoeless statement?" Her eyes travel up and down in silent judgement.

"Ah, of course. It wasn't by choice, you see, my collection has been thoroughly chewed on and eaten by a faceless culprit.

Estelle gasps. "Not a single one was spared?"

"Not a one." Ainsley laughs. "I figured there wasn't much point wearing something with that many holes in it, so. Here we are."

"Oh no, we're so *not*. Not on my watch." She shakes a finger and guides Ainsley by the shoulder. "Come on, get inside and you can try some of my shoes."

"Estelle —"

"*Tut tut tut*, I won't hear it. They're yours."

Estelle's style is not exactly similar to Ainsley's, but she did keep a few comfortable pairs around for the occasional hike with her family. She brings them down to the living room, where Ainsley sits by the long dinner table, overlooking a tall window as the last rays of sunlight fade away. The interior is just as dark as the exterior walls, only well-lit and colourfully decorated. But Ainsley finds it suspiciously quiet for the amount of witches that, at least, used to live here.

"Where are Lucille and Rowland? Is the rest of your coven still here?" She finishes tying the lace of a pair of calf-length boots. Perfect.

"Oh, Ma took them two and the rest down south and they merged with a bigger coven a couple months after your hibernation. I went with too, but once I married Ian we both decided our kids needed a lot of nature for their shifting. So we moved right back in. It's just us now." She looks over Ainsley's shoulder with a wicked smile as someone new joins them. "Speaking of the devil."

Ian looks like the definition of a friendly face, a smile beaming as soon as he realises they have guests over, even if he seems a bit nervous at the surprise of it. The delicate arabesque embroidered along his shirt's collar complements the thick glasses frames resting on his nose.

"You must be Ainsley." He extends a hand. "A pleasure to finally meet you. I'm just grabbing my keys, we'll be out of your hair."

"Oh, of course." Ainsley could not have realised before, but now she sees the faintest light starting to peek in the horizon against the night sky. She takes his handshake. "I hope you and your children have a wonderful night out."

He grabs the keys and gives Estelle a goodbye kiss before leaving. She sees them through the windowpane, Ian gathering their children in the front garden — the tween she had met earlier, and a younger one that looks much more like Ian, but cannot seem to stand still for a second.

"Are you not joining them, Estelle? I would hate to keep you from a family gathering like this." Ainsley begins, but Estelle rolls her eyes.

"Oh, I'm not made for camping like you and Ian are, darling, and you know it. No, I'm much better here." She shudders at the thought of mud and bugs as her bed. "Besides, it's their bonding time so Ian can teach them the ropes of wolf life and whatnot. I'll get my time once they're older and they can work the herbs and candles properly."

Ainsley hums.

"I'm glad you found yourself, Estelle. You have built something beautiful here. I am almost jealous."

Estelle cackles. "'Almost' my ass. Look, I'm so happy you're back, don't get me wrong, dear. But it won't be different this time, I think. If it weren't for my children, I'm not even sure I'd be so close either."

Ainsley straightens her posture in discomfort, being seen so openly, but refuses to look at her.

"Make your point, Estelle."

She lets out an exasperated sigh.

"Look, I know you can't move. But what's keeping you from doing just what I did? Finding someone you like, think of settling down. Hell, with the space you have, you could have five lovers and still never worry about a thing other than keeping them all pampered."

Silence.

"What kept you before?"

Ainsley looks back at her, and Estelle seems uncharacteristically serious.

For a moment, she dares not bring the thought into words. Estelle is her best friend, and this problem is not something she should be burdened with, at least not yet.

Not yet.

But Estelle does not give, her expression stern but her eyes plagued with genuine worry, which hurts Ainsley even more.

"How many years has it been, Estelle?"

Estelle is taken aback by the question.

"What—what do you mean? Why does it even matter?"

"Since I went to sleep that winter, how many years has it been, Estelle?" Ainsley's words are soft, but her eyes are locked on her, waiting for that answer.

Estelle hesitates but concedes.

"Seventeen."

Seventeen years. No one can be asked to wait this long for someone, especially not a life partner. Ainsley would never do such a horrible thing, and Estelle knows it.

"But that was that, wasn't it? It's done, and you're back now. You're here! And you'll be here next year too. Back to your regular internal clock, right?"

Ainsley looks back at the moon, now fully out over the horizon, hovering over the treeline below the hill.

"…Right?"

"I don't know."

She doesn't face Estelle again. She knows if she does, she won't be able to finish saying what she needs to say.

"I… I don't remember when I first took this form. The tree… Well, it has always been there, that I do know. But what I do remember is the curiosity I felt when I first saw creatures roaming this same forest. The freedom of walking, the possibilities of that life. And, well, the rest is history. Many, many lifetimes worth of history.

But the truth is, this isn't the first big pause in my walking life. First, it was just a longer winter than usual.

Then, an entire year skipped, just like that, gone. Now…
Well. You're aware."

"What are you telling me, Ainsley, darling?" Estelle
extends a hand across the table, holding Ainsley's in her own.

She lets out a nervous laughter.

"Honestly, I am not sure myself. It could be a pattern,
it could be just an atypical period in my existence. There's
no manual guide I ought to consult, no wiser one I can go
to and ask. There's only… Me."

Estelle shakes her head furiously and squeezes her hand.

"I'm right here, aren't I, darling? And sure, sure, I have
no idea how your inner machine works but what I do know
is that for now, you're back. To me, that's enough cause for
a big celebration, don't you think? In fact!"

Estelle produces a small device from her pockets, a sort
of palm-sized screen that she taps and taps continuously,
leaving Ainsley in perplexed silence.

"We'll do just that, a big party to celebrate our
esteemed elder and good friend, Ainsley, for being back
among us poor mortal souls! How does that sound?"

Estelle nudges Ainsley by the shoulders, and she laughs
at the absurdity of a party being thrown in her honour.

"What am I now, a groundhog? Do you hear yourself?"

"Oh, just work with me here, dear. I remember
you saying something about a festival you would host
yourself, didn't you? Every May, after you would come out
of hibernation, with flowers and food and drinks. What
was it again?"

"May Day?"

Estelle snaps her fingers. "That's the one."

"True, I did host it, long ago. But Estelle, we have missed the deadline for this. The first of the month is days past us."

"So? It's only the eight, we still have the rest of spring. We'll schedule for the end of the month instead and just call it, I don't know… Uh…"

Ainsley raises an eyebrow.

"May Eve."

"Please."

But Estelle is set, and once she has decided something, few can stop her. Perhaps Ainsley, but even then. She has a smug grin and looks expectantly at her.

"So, what do you say? Are you in? Don't worry, I'll organise it since it is my idea — and, well it's also what I do for a living so you'll have the best of the best. I'll get the company I work for in this, it will be done in a blink, you'll see."

Ainsley takes a deep breath as Estelle sits there, device in hand. No, she does not feel safe letting a company handle something so delicate like a festival for her community — much less May Day — but she trusts Estelle.

She supposes that will have to be enough.

"Very well! I'm in." Ainsley throws her hands up in defeat. "But make sure to invite everyone, will you? I want it to be memorable, for all of us."

If this is to be goodbye, then let it be memorable.

Estelle's smirk is devious.

"Now we're talking." She brings her strange device to her ear and begins talking to someone on it — presumably another employee of the aforementioned company.

Oh! *Mobile* telephone. What a nifty thing.

Gosh, Ainsley can scarcely believe it. She wakes one day, expecting it will be just another year of empty halls and sleepless nights. And perhaps it will be. Perhaps she does have another isolating year ahead of her. But now with the promise of a single evening where she can expect to lose sleep over something other than anxiety.

Is it a mistake? It most definitely feels like one. Yet Estelle gestures excitedly on the phone, already figuring out catering, music, a mental map of the sitting disposition around the tree, centrepieces, et cetera.

Wait.

"What locale did you suggest again for this event, Estelle?" Ainsley interrupts.

Estelle brings a hand to her phone for a moment, tilting her head in Ainsley's direction.

"Well, your house, of course. Plenty of space, darling. You won't be alone for a second this month, I can promise you now."

Stranger company. Lovely. At least she seems to be tactile enough to request magical folk only working on this project.

No glamours. Small blessings.

Ainsley, however, gets no time to ruminate further or plan her following disrupted weeks. A long howl, of the same pitch and tone as the one she heard earlier as she made her way over, resonates outside. Estelle wastes no time and swings open the front door, Ainsley right in toe.

It's dark outside, but against the moonlight, the faint silhouette of a wolf cub emerges from the bushes surrounding the garden, jingling keys in his tiny mouth.

Ian's keys.

"One second, dear." Estelle slumps and mutes her phone again. "Young man, what are you doing back here!? Go back to your Pa right this instant, or else!"

The wolf yelps and scurries back into the shadows as fast as it came. Ainsley cannot contain it and breaks her polite silence to laugh.

She decides any worrying thoughts can wait, and with a grumbling stomach and preoccupied Estelle, dinner prep begs her attention. She has a bag full of a delicious bounty just waiting to be turned into a bowl of filling salad. She takes the bag to the kitchen and starts washing the ingredients.

Tonight, nature has provided, and she shall be forever grateful.

# Chapter 2

A kettle cries on the stove, steam rapidly evaporating into nothingness. The fabric filter waits impatiently, ground beans and sugar ready to blend. The aroma of coffee is so present the beverage might as well be ready and served, sitting in a delicate teacup on the balcony table.

Yet it remains there, undone.

Priscilla should have remedied this five minutes ago, while there was still enough water left for at least a cup on her way to work. But it has now been ten minutes and she stands there, immovable, entranced by the soft hues of gold and pink outside of the small window of her flat's kitchen. A flock of birds cuts the tinted clouds, undoubtedly on their way back from a long winter's emigration.

She wonders what it would be like to fly so freely like that. In her mind's eye, she sees it too, wings sprouting from her back — in a moment, she is no longer Priscilla, but a majestic creature of nature. An angelic presence, dappled fabric around her body flows behind her in an ethereal trail, her skin now of dark marble with cracks of silver and gold, her hair pinned up and adorned by laurels. The white flock circles her as she twirls, an unending dance against the misty air. Unbound by borders, papers, schedules — they are above it all.

She would land with this entourage of majestic creatures, then, on a lake overseeing a castle. The people of the village would celebrate the good word of her arrival, ask her of her adventures, invite her over to catch up and bless their household with her magic. She would do it, of course, and in turn, paint them a picture of a great threat to the west — two mighty dragons she outmatched with nothing more than her words and wits.

She would spare no detail — All the benefits, all the dangers, all the emotions her adventures had brought her. Ah! The wind against her face on those long flights alone would be worth it…

But as rapidly as it started, the daydream also ends.

Suddenly aware again, she remembers herself — her satin bonnet and matching nightgown against her skin, her cold hands resting against the light wood of the counter, her fluffy slippers against the panelling of her kitchen's floor. Her doe eyes are brought into focus again, the steam rising in front of her clouding her vision and bringing her back to her task.

One left unfinished, and now lost.

It's instinctual — her shoulders tense, and she turns her stove off as fast as she can. She readies for someone as real as her make-believe enemies to come and scold her for the ruined breakfast they were so looking forward to.

And she waits.

And waits.

And when they never come, she lets out a long sigh, looking around to an empty home — but a home nonetheless.

Her home.

In. Out. The world won't end.

She looks back to the ingredients and realises that, despite her thoughts screaming otherwise, she can deal with it later.

She has been curating every nook and cranny of this space, slowly adding to her collection of vintage furniture and handmade lace decor, of unfinished DIY projects and fabric plants after one too many casualties. Over the course of the four years she has lived here, she has successfully taken a drab rental of white walls to something akin to a slice of a fairy book princess's room, a small part of her fantasies made true.

She makes her way to her bedroom, revelling in the tint of the sunrise that makes its way through the linen curtains, grounding herself with every step. The light dapples on her canopy bed, all the way to her open closet just at the end of the slanted ceiling — the one accented with flowery fairy lights she installed with her own two hands and a rickety set of stairs. She browses her collection of self-made and thrifted dresses in pastels and creams, of thick heels and ballet flats, and her small box of jewellery — one of the few things she managed to keep from her old life before she had to flee. It's still one of her most prized possessions, a reminder of a different Priscilla, a younger one.

She would have been so proud; so happy.

She grabs her phone from the nightstand and quickly sends an audio message as she picks her outfit for the day.

*It happened again. Meet me in half an hour?*

She doesn't wait for an answer as she's sure Orion will be there at their usual spot - a tiny cafe in a secluded street at the heart of their city. It was Orion's favourite spot ever since it opened years before Priscilla moved here, and now she has made it her own as well.

"Alright, no use feeling down about it, time to start the day!" She pats her cheeks, trying to keep herself awake.

There's much to be done in reality.

Half an hour passes and Priscilla is out of the door. Despite losing so much time, she refuses to face the day without her armour — donned in an almost-sheer white shirt with frilly neck and cuffs, a pencil skirt in blush and sensible heels, she haphazardly stuffs her possessions into her handbag before locking the door and running to her car.

She doesn't necessarily need to dress up — her job as a freelance event decorator allows her to work from home in her pyjamas if need be; and even if she needs to run to a location or a shop, there's no uniform or dress code imposed on her.

In fact, Priscilla knows that the way she dresses —
in clothes of eras bygone, frills and pastels and delicate
jewellery to tie it all together — only puts a target on her
back for scrutinising eyes at best, and ill intention at worst.
She is aware of the choices she makes every day while
looking like her.

Maybe a pair of jeans and a basic
T-shirt would be safer.

*No, no, look like a clown
all you want.*

*Make a scene.*
*Dig your own grave.*
*See if I care.*

She catches this foreign
thought out of the corner of her
mind before she internalises
it, shaking it off.

It doesn't matter. She
knows. But she has come
to enjoy those clothes,
make a home out of them
just as she made her home in her
own body, despite what the world
kept telling her about it. Just
how she had made a home in
this town, out of nothing.

And none of it
would have been possible
without Orion.

She finds him sitting by a table outside, a drink in hand - a bright can of a weird energy juice she has never heard of before and doesn't care enough to ask about. But more importantly, she also finds a nice cup of coffee waiting for her, warm and inviting in this chilly morning.

"Orion, love of my life, my beacon of hope in this sad, sad existence! How much do I owe you?" She hugs him tightly, taking his neck into her arms, draining him of breath in a cuteness aggression attack.

"Ach, c'mon Pri, it's too early for all this. Drink the damn thing and thank me later." He pats her lock on him in defeat as he gasps for air. She concedes, for now, and sits opposite the table.

Orion's deep eye bags contrast with the kindness of his gaze. He's always been a grumpy guy, with his signature leather jacket and a spiky bracelet Priscilla has never seen him take off. They've been friends since high school — two awkward teenagers trying to find themselves, bonding over their love of fashion, underrated bands and raw political ideas, exchanging messages on a forum board that is now long dead. He was the first and only to offer a helping hand after Priscilla abandoned her old household all those years back, her 'real' friends having turned their backs on her as soon as she was no longer a person of interest to them.

So she gathered what little she had for a plane ticket and took a leap of faith.

Orion was there for her as she hunted for a new job, a new home, a new life, as she crashed on his couch, just as she had been there for him as he figured out his identity and tried to navigate the medical system. They've been inseparable ever since, and despite both being quite busy in their careers lately — Priscilla with her many events on every side of this city, and Orion with his boutique — They would always make time to meet every so often by this exact table.

"Let's hope the coffee turns your morning around." He adds, concerned. "How bad was it?"

He's asking about the sudden bout of daydreaming earlier, of course. Priscilla tenses again.

"Not as bad as it could have been. I didn't burn the house down if that's what you're asking." She scrunches her face in a taunt as soon as she senses judgement coming from him, all in playful banter. "Just a good half an hour looking at the sunrise, dreaming of flying with the swans as they make their way back from winter. Vanquishing dragons, mingling with some medieval peeps. It's kinda poetic if you think about it."

Priscilla raises her hands as if painting a picture for him. But he doesn't 'think about it', seeing right through her deflection, and patiently raises an eyebrow, tired eyes unmoving.

"Fine, it wasn't so poetic when I realised all the water I had in my kettle just dissipated."

He raises it higher.

"…And when I realised I had no time left for a proper meal. Don't look at me like that! I grabbed a protein bar before I left, I'll have it at some point before lunch. I promise."

"Good." He takes a last sip of his can and chucks it into the public bin behind him. "Next time just tell me, I'll buy you a bagel or something."

"I will." She finishes her drink as well, dabs her mouth with a napkin and throws her bag around her shoulder, shrugging. "For all that it's worth, they are happening less. Baby steps, right?"

He closes his eyes and nods; it's progress, he recognises. The daydreaming would consume hours of her day at a time earlier in her life, keeping her from school, from home, from being a perfect daughter. Now she's finally at a point where they are few and far between, only a fast glimpse that would force her to skip a meal or two instead of sitting immovable on her bed, rocking back and forth until someone finds her.

Therapy helped. Orion helped. She worked hard on her own for it as well.

Yet… She feels the loss of it too. The worlds she created in her mind's eye were real for her, a haven from the chaos of everyday life where she was safe, if only for a moment.

And almost selfishly, no matter how much better her reality has become, how she has made it much more enticing for herself… She doesn't want the fantasy to be forgotten and discarded. Not all of it, at least, when it helped her so much.

Could she keep it, maybe for just a while longer? Put it in her jewellery box, a keepsake, a memento of a locket pendant with a picture of that part of her life. Warded by dragon scale and covered in pixie dust. To be looked at only when in complete privacy, to remember, to cherish — but to be able to put the worst of it behind.

She only wishes for it's safety as well.

# Chapter 3

vent planning can be so boring sometimes.

Even after specialising in the decoration part only, leaving behind any sort of nightmarish struggle involving scheduling, some days… Well, some days all you get to do is sit in your room and answer emails. Make phone calls. Wait for deliveries to be made.

Funny enough, Priscilla wishes today was that kind of day. A nice, simple 'nothing is happening, please somebody do something, oh God' kind of day.

Instead, she arrives back home late at night, arms and hands full of bags upon bags from her various trips to stores all around town — craft, hardware, textile. She's pretty sure there has been glitter stuck to her face throughout the entire day from swatching for the perfect colour to put in her heat gun. At this point, she doesn't care any more.

Let it shine, let them look, it's done.

She struggles with the weight through the door, but as soon as it closes behind her she collapses on the ground, letting go of this burden. She looks into the bags, disarranged and thrown around, and all she can see is a sea of greys and neutrals.

How did it end up like this again? The location was perfect for rich reds and complex golds, a historical building that had been renovated pristinely within the past decade and now housed a luxury hotel that had been rented for the occasion. It was inspiring, really, to step foot in such a place where the real Priscilla would never have and never will belong. But before, she would have had constant fantasies about attending a royal ball in a building just like that one, dressed in satins and silks — she would have been a princess in this, at her coronation, awaiting the perfect face in the dancing crowd to snatch her away in a waltz and swoon her heart with poetic promises —

Her mind reeled that afternoon, building the stage internally over what she saw there and already making plans, only to rudely be stopped in her tracks.

'The client requested the same colours of their branding. Something classy, but not old. Make it work.'

Her blood boiled, but in true Priscilla fashion, she simply smiled and nodded politely. 'Happy thoughts, happy thoughts.' Why didn't they rent a more modern building, then?— 'Happy thoughts!'

So here she lies, in the dullest sea of materials she could find and absolutely no idea of how to proceed.

The vintage clock on her wall rings the hour, and she battles her need for both food and rest. Her eyes land on her kitchen counter and then her soft couch, in much closer reach, and a clear winner emerges. She musters up just enough energy to dig her phone from her bag in the mess and wastes no time plopping down to order something for dinner, kicking her shoes to the side.

She will make it work. That's what she does.

Midway through her mindless scrolling for food, however, she's interrupted by an email. A work email, of course, probably for another dull company party celebrating another pointless quarterly achievement.

Dismissed. That's a problem for tomorrow's Priscilla. Today's Priscilla gets to enjoy some king prawn fried rice to another rewatch of Pride and Prejudice.

Yet now snuggled up to her hand-crocheted fuzzy throw, her mind wanders back to that nagging email waiting for her in her inbox.

Fine.

Curiosity takes hold and she opens the damn thing. Her eyes dart over the lines as she rises from her spot on the couch in excitement. The details are fuzzy, and instead of an address, she gets a location on a map. Weird. But, right at the bottom, an image is attached. An image that sets the deal for her instantly.

Oh, she should have one hundred percent read this earlier.

Priscilla might yet get to bring to life the vision of her dreams.

The photo did not do it justice. This place is *gorgeous*.

Made of the same stone material as some of the older buildings in town, this place is different. Huge, majestic, inspiring? Yes, of course. But the way nature wraps itself around this structure, flowering ivy and roses and wisteria making a nest around the many arched windows in a warm hug. Birds she has never heard sing before surround it and a cool breeze with the sound of running water suggests a river somewhere not too far.

Standing there and experiencing this vista makes the difficult path worth it. Orion was kind enough to give her a ride for most of the way, but when the path became too narrow for a car, she reluctantly took the challenge of hiking the final dozen feet.

He tried to stop her, in fact, and almost succeeded. He had heard strange stories about this mansion hidden in the woods — the last owner was an eccentric man who mysteriously disappeared without a trace a whole two decades ago, give or take. Orion and his mates would play around this area as children and they all could swear it was haunted.

One of them broke in then, trying to prove his courage to the rest of their friend group — but came back a quarter hour later with his pants pissed clean. Crossed his heart he could hear a voice coming from the ceiling. After that, they never came anywhere close again, just in case some vengeful ghost was out for guts.

A part of Priscilla was terrified after that tale, she admits. But another could not keep away — she had to see what was up there for herself. Whoever had moved in probably just wanted to celebrate their new life in a new house, and if she could help make that a memorable day, she wanted to.

So she promises to keep him updated and makes peace with a potential abduction and/or possession.

Oh God was she wrong though — delightfully so.

As soon as she swings one of the double front doors open, she knows she is in for an adventure.

First, she sees the beauty of the outside walls reflected in kind inside, but within a surprising structure as she steps into a distinctively Moroccan style layout. A large patio with plenty more budding flora scattered between rock and ground; and the many rooms on both floors encasing it inside, connected by delicately carved rails and curved staircases on both sides.

Second, at the heart of all of this, a birch tree like none she has seen before; its canopy reaching far above the roof, spiralling over it in a second layer of protection, green leaves dotted by orange flowering.

And third, right behind its trunk, she spots Estelle of all people, in conversation with someone still obscured from this angle.

Priscilla has worked with her before on a couple of other projects and found her equal parts skilled, dependable and terrifying. She's glad to see a familiar face, however, and is happy to know this will be coordinated well. But what catches her eye in this moment more than anything else is —

It can't be. A trick of light.

Priscilla tries to convince herself all she sees is a low-hanging branch, this weird perspective against her vision. It has to be.

But then the branch *moves*. It reaches for Estelle's shoulder, and a deep, melodic voice comes from it, echoing like a lullaby.

Her heart skips a beat, but Priscilla isn't scared. She finds herself entranced, lost for words as she steps closer and closer. Slowly, bright green vines for hair, dark-tinted lips and a swirling black void are revealed as they lock eyes with her for the briefest of moments — before Estelle notices her presence and entirely blocks Priscilla's line of sight.

She comes with a firm handshake and a bit too much energy. With the contact, something gets in Priscilla's eye and she instinctively goes to rub it for relief. Estelle tries to greet her and start a conversation, but she registers nothing.

She recovers from the blinking, shaking her head, and looks back to where that figure stood a second before. Instead of the curious sight, she meets with a much more mundane vision, but just as awe-inspiring.

Standing an entire foot or two taller than Priscilla, a woman greets her with a serene smile. Fragrant of petrichor and wild apples, her pale skin is thoroughly freckled, her caramel eyes framed by long locks of auburn curls. A sage green shawl keeps a hand occupied and her pose exudes well-earned authority.

"It is a pleasure to make your acquaintance, Priscilla. Please, call me Ainsley. Welcome to my home."

She introduces herself with a long handshake, but Priscilla doesn't need the verbal confirmation — Ainsley looks like she was made for this place.

A fairytale queen worthy of a fairytale castle.

"Priscilla! Priscilla Cardoso. But you know that. Ah." God, she's glad her complexion hides the flush under her skin so well right now. "I'll take good care of it, I promise. I'm here to make this festival unforgettable for you."

Ainsley chuckles politely. "You already have."

"Well!" Estelle comes into focus again and guides Priscilla away from her death by embarrassment. "Why don't you do the rounds, darling, start your brainstorming and whatnot while I finish discussing all the details with Ainsley? We'll be closing upstairs for the guests, but the patio and the gardens will need your touch, alright?"

Priscilla is hesitant, still looking over her shoulder for any traces of that figure, still a bit shaken and confused. She doesn't think twice before following Estelle's suggestion and getting lost in the state's premises, leaving the two alone again.

Just Estelle, Ainsley, the secret that was almost revealed.

❧

Ainsley catches Estelle by her arms not a moment too soon, offering her a shoulder for support and taking her to the living room a few metres away. She closes the door behind them, and she guides her friend to the closest sofa she can find.

"Darling, that was a close call." Estelle heaves. Using her magic with no preparation like that would take its toll on even the strongest witch.

"Indeed it was." Thankfully Estelle was able to catch Priscilla's presence in time to place a glamour spell over her eyes.

There are not exactly any hard laws in regards to creatures such as Ainsley and Estelle to keep their nature

33

a secret from others. But throughout the years, guidelines emerged from experience, to keep mass hysteria or hunts from ever happening again. With how many creatures of magic live amongst humans, befriending them, falling in love… Sooner or later the truth must come to the surface, shared only for one more soul to keep it, sworn to their deathbed.

Trust is key here, and Priscilla currently is nothing more than Estelle's work acquaintance at best, and a total stranger to Ainsley at worst.

Yet Ainsley cannot stop pondering about that look. In that split second when their eyes met, and the truth was laid bare, not yet ripe… Ainsley has had her fair share of encounters just like this. Lost hikers, ghost hunters, curious teenagers — it was never her intention to become the creature of legends, of fae folk tales people would spin about the forest's denizens.

All she would do was silently step into their wavering lamp light. We all fear what we do not know, and then all it would take was that split moment where they would be faced with uncertainty. Not a single word uttered, and they would be gone, running in terror.

But Priscilla's look, then…

Ainsley could not see any shock, hesitation, or horror. Her eyes…

They almost *sparkled*.

Wonder.

"Who is she?" Ainsley asks.

"Priscilla? Oh, I can't tell you much — she's an independent contractor, a decorator we hire sometimes. We've worked together for a few projects in the past and she was a sweetheart, don't get me wrong, but a bit spacey too. I guess that's just her process — you know how those creative types are."

That, unfortunately, does not answer any of the many questions Ainsley has about this woman.

"Correct me if I'm wrong, but I was under the impression you specifically requested magical folk only to your company."

"I did." Estelle is almost offended.

"Then how did this happen?"

They both scurry their minds to the night before, to the phone call that sealed the deal on Estelle's end of the bargain, and they both get to it at the same time.

"Your son."

"Oh dear, yes. I was told our in-house decorator was on paternity leave, that we had to get a contractor. And I told my assistant: "Don't get Priscilla, get Daniel.""

"Right as you were interrupted. Could it really have been that?"

"Oh yes, Kyle is easily flustered. A scream like that, even over the phone would have shaken him just enough for a mix-up."

So a simple accident almost resulted in an entire scene, right at her house. Estelle did promise this following month to be eventful, but Ainsley did not for a single moment expect this level of excitement.

"It's a shame too, Priscilla would be perfect for this festival — I've seen her portfolio, it's all florals and frills. But it is for the best. I'm sorry, I'll explain everything and get Daniel in her place by tomorrow."

Estelle gets up from the sofa, a bit less drained now, and opens the door, undoubtedly on her way to find Priscilla and cut her ties to this festival. But Ainsley follows her, catching her arm before she does.

"Wait."

"Wait?" Estelle looks back, confused.

She's right, it would be for the best. Ainsley herself, in a different circumstance, would wholeheartedly agree with her and their plans would continue with no other hiccups.

But she hesitates.

"…Let me talk to her. You have already glamoured her vision, which will also keep her from seeing other magical folk of more unique figures like me. She might still work."

Estelle tilts her head, and Ainsley knows what she wants to say, even without words. 'This isn't like you, Ainsley. What's going on, darling?'

Ainsley clears her throat. "Just… Let me have a few words. There's no need to dismiss her before even talking. If after that I still find her unacceptable, I will explain the situation myself."

"Hm." Estelle thinks for a moment. "Alright, alright! But that glamour will barely last a day, I just had no time to cast it. I'll swing by later tonight with the proper thing. For you and some housewards as well, just in case."

"That's way too much — we are not even sure if we will need it long term yet." Ainsley crosses her arms.

Estelle cackles. "Call it a hunch, dear."

She makes for her bag and coat she had left by the door as Ainsley shows her out.

"I do have a lot to put in place if we want to make our deadline though, so I'll leave you to it, alright?"

And with that, it's just Ainsley, Priscilla, and possibility left.

Priscilla doesn't know what to make of the past few minutes. She sits with her thoughts for a bit, trying to make sense, any sense, of what had just happened.

Nothing. Not even Orion, after scaring her with all the ghost stories, would believe a single word out of her mouth about this. She still shoots him a message anyway, just confirming all her extremities are still attached to her body. But she can't say the same about her heart.

Ainsley. Ainsley… what again? If she had a surname, Priscilla didn't catch it in her stupor. Partly because of the weird situation before, but also, well…

She's sublime. A particular kind of beauty, almost otherworldly.

In the eight years Priscilla has lived here, romance hasn't quite crossed her mind that often. Her first years were survival mode only, her trying to get a life made in a new place, which barely left any time for anything else. This doesn't mean it hasn't happened since — with a bit more time lately, she has taken a few shots in the dating pool. All wonderful women — but none of them *clicked*.

Ah, what is she even thinking here? Priscilla barely knows Ainsley. Is she even available? Would Ainsley be even remotely interested in her? Besides, she's here to provide a service to Ainsley, and even if indirectly, hitting on the person who has hired you isn't exactly workplace-appropriate behaviour, is it?

So she focuses on that instead, trying to clear her head of any distracting thoughts by taking some photos and doing what she does best.

Which comes to her so easily, too. Walking through this place is like wandering in so many of her daydream scenarios. The backyard is just as beautiful as the front of the house — but instead of the sea of flowers, it houses a vast vegetable garden with fruit trees of all sorts encasing it, perfectly blending into the forest ahead. Here and there she finds a couple of swings and a treehouse to the side.

It's a funny detail Priscilla finally places. With a mansion this big, usually the owned land around it is miles and miles wide, golf courses and lavish pools, heavily protected by thick external walls and personnel.

But she has not seen the sight of a single fence yet, not now, not on her way in either. It's as if this house sits hidden away, the forest itself her backyard and protector.

Oh, what Priscilla wouldn't do to live in a place just like this. Maybe, ideally, closer to town and her friends, but still… The faint white noise of the river she can hear ever clearer now would lull her to sleep every night, the magnolias would greet her every morning. Not even her grey thumb of death would put a dent into this bounty of a garden.

It will never happen, not in this lifetime. The council tax alone would bankrupt her to the ground. Besides…

She looks back to the mansion, two tall stories of it imposing over her — the birch inside even more so as it peeks over the roof.

Must be awfully quiet to live alone in all this, so isolated from everything.

Her feelings aside, she hopes Ainsley has someone to share her nights with in this place.

"Are you enjoying the view?"

Ainsley stands right by Priscilla's side, hunching slightly to quietly announce herself amidst Priscilla's musings. She yelps in fright, jumping in place.

"Oh, God! I didn't see you there."

Ainsley revels a bit too much at the expected outcome, but her smile is nothing but polite.

"I did not mean to shake you so. I apologise."

"Oh." Priscilla picks up none of it. "You're fine. I was just deep in my thoughts and didn't see you coming at all."

Ainsley hums. "Am I safe to assume you were making plans for how you intend to reshape my home for the festival?

"Yes, you would!"

Priscilla claps in excitement and produces a device from her shoulder bag, much like the mobile Estelle used to make that fated call yesterday. This one, however, is much bigger, barely fitting in said bag. A unique pen sits attached to its side as Priscilla touches the screen to reveal a series of photos she has taken of Ainsley's estate.

Over most of them, quick little scribbles have been sketched in hasty but confident lines.

"I know I don't have the best drawing skills, but these are some of the ideas just off the top of my head. Thoughts?"

Ainsley takes a closer look, holding it in her hands now. It's a picture of her patio, taken from somewhere on the second floor, overlooking her soul tree. Over it, in red lines, a quick disposition of sitting areas of stick tables, chairs and benches fill the otherwise empty area. And, most notably, draped over the stairs and railings of the second floor, a tapestry of flora cascades down, sheer fabric accenting any blank spots in the composition. She also sees a buffet display and a tower of crystal champagne glasses along the halls.

"Did you plan all of this already?" Ainsley is surprised. Priscilla has barely been here for a quarter hour.

"Too much?" She takes the device back and holds it against her heart. "To be honest, I don't know much about May Day, it's not really a thing in my home country. And from what I saw in the briefing, you're hosting this for your family and friends only, so the plan is a cosy atmosphere for them, not a lavish royal ball, but…"

She takes a step back, ravelling in her surroundings again.

"Well, as soon as I stepped in, my mind just took the reins and I couldn't stop it! I guess I got carried away."

A soft breeze sways her hair then, and Ainsley takes a moment to see Priscilla properly now. Her tight curls are pulled back neatly on top of her head, held together by a lilly-adorned comb. The ruffles of her dress shirt billows and her smooth sepia skin is powdered by delicate makeup around her eyes and cheeks. Her smile is ever present, but her topaz eyes reflect their distance, looking out a thousand miles away. Ainsley is almost sure she's about to lose Priscilla to her own world — but after a minute she pulls herself back to the garden they stand on, facing Ainsley with that same wonder-infused gaze.

Ainsley is the one to almost lose herself now.

"You have a lovely home, Ms…"

"Oh, none of that, please. Titles like that have never sat well with me — just Ainsley will do fine."

"Ainsley, then." Priscilla's smile brightens.

She nods in agreement and tries to bring them both back into the task at hand. "It's incredible, by the way. The design. I'm pleasantly surprised by how much you're already figured out in such a small window of time, but I do have some concerns."

"Oh?" Priscilla tries to show Ainsley her sketches again, but Ainsley's hand stops her, bringing her device back down to her chest.

"However — it is almost noon, and what kind of host would I be if I didn't offer you a spot of tea? We can go over all the details then." She offers, extending a hand back to the mansion.

Priscilla has done her damn best so far to keep it cool and professional around Ainsley, but she's only human. And, technically, this is still for work, yes, but she cannot help feeling her cheeks heat all over again at the offer of lunch.

"That'd… That'd be really nice. Thank you."

Turns out, Priscilla missed a big part of what makes May Day, well, May Day. She should have researched a bit more of the history behind it instead of jumping the gun and going straight for the photos.

In every image she could find, she would see the iconic Maypole with its colourful ribbons wrapped around it. Children, dancing in a circle, effectively braiding the pole as they twirl in a pattern. She swears she has seen it in a couple of movies too.

But now that Ainsley has set her down and explained it to her, she also knows it was a festival to celebrate spring and the coming of summer, that it used to be far more popular a few centuries ago amongst the common folk, and that it now, unfortunately, barely leaves the classroom.

"The Maypole you saw is a more recent creation, something easier to move around a settlement. But when you're someone out in the forest, well… Any tree with enough space around it will do." Ainsley explains as she finishes pouring the tea into the ceramic teacups, and through the open door of the kitchen, she looks at herself.

Priscilla connects the dots easily.

"Oh, the birch in your patio." It makes perfect sense to her now. The birch tree will be the May Pole, as it always has been before. No need for a double to be placed outside. "How old is it? I've never seen one this tall, not even in pictures." She asks, trying to mask her strong interest.

"Older than I am, by aeons." Which isn't a lie, but it still pains Ainsley to have to skirt around the truth with a vague answer. "It was here before this building was constructed, and my one true hope is that it will still be here by the time I'm no longer around and it all crumbles back into dust."

A sadness flashes across Ainsley's face then, Priscilla notices, but she doesn't pry.

"Oh, that's incredible. How long have you been hosting the festival?" She asks.

"For as far as I can remember. My community is one of the few that still celebrates May Day, you see. A lot of us have a special tie with these woods, so it's a sacred event for us, even when all we can afford to do is a simple gathering.

Those are usually the best if I'm honest. Just a small band of fools, drinking and dancing around a tree into the wee hours of the night." She gives a nostalgic chuckle after taking a sip of her tea, and Priscilla nods. "But even now, our numbers dwindle. So many people I know have detached themselves from their roots. They've left the forest completely."

Ainsley must really care for her own. Priscilla wonders what kind of community she has fostered here, one so close to nature. Some sort of religious practice, for sure. Pagan, perhaps, or some sort of witchcraft like Orion's sister does.

"It's a shame, huh? I get it, though. With how busy everyone is nowadays, it's so hard to make time for getting together like that, just for a laugh if nothing else." Priscilla reminisces on the many times she was invited for a night out with her friends, or a potluck at Orion's, but work got in the way. Or she would find herself too tired for anything after, just like yesterday was. It's a hard balance to keep, and so many times we don't even get a choice at all.

Ainsley is almost surprised to see somewhat eye to eye with Priscilla, expecting her to downplay it like so many humans that she had met before throughout the years. But she doesn't, offering an honest comment in earnest, and Ainsley hums in agreement.

They sit for a moment in contemplation of their situation until Priscilla shifts in her seat, and takes another sip of her drink before going back to their plans.

"So, I was right then, you just need something smaller for a night amongst friends? I'll be happy to scale it down for you." She says, ready to start over with her sketches.

But Ainsley shakes her head, that same sadness making itself present again. "Not this time… This might be the last opportunity for me to host May Day in a while…"

She looks over to the other part of her soul again, letting herself feel for a moment if only to bounce back faster from the pain.

"So I want to have one last night with every single person I can manage to fit into this house, one last time. And for that, I will need the best I can find on that task, and that seems to be you, Priscilla. Are you up for it?" She asks, making her decision final.

The compliment ought to make Priscilla flustered like a teenager again, but her pride in her work is stronger. She rolls over her sleeves in a metaphor and agrees enthusiastically.

"Leave it to me."

# Chapter 4

"What, you're telling me you have a thing for the ghost of Birchwood Cairn?" Orion can barely contain his hysterical laughter, his car swaying in the dirt path as he loses focus.

It has been a few days since Priscilla's first visit to Ainsley's mansion, and this is not the reaction she was expecting from Orion after she'd promised she'd tell him more next time he drives her there.

"Not a ghost, Orion, just Ainsley, the owner — and as far as I know, the only person living there." She just happens to be good-looking, is all.

"OK, and who's this almighty Ainsley you won't shut up about?" He's obviously teasing, but Priscilla can see his curiosity clear as day in that question.

Oh, you *gossip*.

Priscilla may be able to lie to Orion, but not to herself. Yes, Ainsley has plagued her mind ever since they've met. Mostly because, again, she is an incredibly attractive woman.

But it's not just that, is it? Priscilla stayed a bit longer after they were both done with tea and their festival discussions, just chatting. She made many more questions to Ainsley than Ainsley did to her, and yet she has the feeling Ainsley is the one that came out of that conversation with all the information, and not her.

Ainsley didn't exactly refrain from answering anything, but Priscilla had the distinct feeling she was hiding information in every sweet message that came out of her peachy lips. Which was really frustrating, because she also felt that they connected then, even if it was for a brief moment.

Perhaps it was just another trick of her heart, just like her vision earlier that day.

"I… I don't know, to be honest. She told me it was her back then, seventeen years ago, living in that mansion, and that it has been in her family forever. She's the only inheritor now, and she seems to only be moving back here for a year, and then she's gone again. Something about business in another place."

"Hold on, hold on, she was the old man that disappeared? Are you telling me this Ainsley is trans too?" Orion is pleasantly surprised by that revelation, a mix of confusion but pride in towards one of his elders until Priscilla shrugs.

"Are you sure it's not your information that's wrong?" Priscilla crosses her arms. You can never trust a story that has been exchanged so many times.

"No, this is the one thing I'm certain of, my mate's uncle would see him come down from the mountain every now and then and strike up some conversation about the highway, and he swears it was a middle-aged guy. My info is solid, trust me."

"Then it couldn't have been Ainsley." That one is a pretty safe bet for Priscilla to make. "Ainsley looks to be in her late thirties now, she would have been younger than us back then. It just doesn't make sense."

The only way for it to be her would be if she was, somehow, forever young — and that scenario would be too out there even for Priscilla. No way.

"Aye, so what's your plan? Keep it casual? Or just do your job and leave, not worth the bother?" Orion asks.

"Oh no, no. I'll ask for her number after work today." Priscilla says primly. She knows what a chance of a lifetime looks like, she's not letting Ainsley go if she can help it.

"What!?" Orion reels, abruptly stopping his car in its tracks. He looks at Priscilla in as much shock as his eyebags let him. "Pri, I know that look. You just said she's leaving in a year. What the fuck are you trying to do, get your heart broken, dumbass?" His words are harsh but they come from a place of familiarity and worry.

Once, Priscilla would have thought exactly like Orion. And to be fair, she appreciates him being the voice of reason to her recklessness — he keeps her in check, and she pushes him to live a little sometimes.

All her life, all that was expected of her was what a proper woman should do. A proper date with a proper man that leads into a proper wedding into a proper picket-fence-children-ever-after. A fantasy, much like one of her own. But this had been implanted into her, an imposition, instead of blooming from the heart.

She was six, and already had her life been planned out for her, by people she thought she could trust.

To hell with that. She isn't even attracted to men, for crying out loud. Not that they understood.

So she did the work, she broke herself and that single future she knew down to bits, and burned them up. From the ashes she rebuilt and learnt how to be a new person. How to be the real Priscilla, the one she had buried six feet under the pressure of her family. A diamond in the rough.

She's catching up on lost time — so what? She deserves something real, for however long she's afforded it.

"Are you jealous I'd choose her over you and move away?" Priscilla teases, bumping into him, but her heart is sincere. "This is my home, Orion, and you're my family. I'd never do that."

"Ach, that's not — I know — Pri!" He's flustered now, which almost seems anachronous to his personality.

"What?" She plays dumb but knows exactly what she's doing.

Orion sighs and throws his hands up in defeat.

"You know what? Fuck it. I'm warning you for nothing." He starts the car and drives again to calm himself down. "You'll get there and if this Ainsley has any brain cells in her banger, she'll say no to you. You'll feel like shit, we'll crash at yours, destroy a tub of ice cream and it will be over in a week, tops."

Priscilla shrugs. She might. But... She might not, as well.

She's already lived for future Priscilla, and she's done. Today's Priscilla deserves happiness now too, Ever After or not.

Orion seems to finally focus on the road, the conversation falling into a comfortable silence for a minute. Until a tentative grin takes his expression as he turns back to Priscilla.

"So… You don't have a thing for a ghost, just a regular old MILF. Got it."

"Orion!" She doesn't dignify that joke with an answer, but his laughter is infectious, and she can't contain her own.

⁖

"What!? Priscilla!? The human!? Our event decorator!?"

"A bit higher, Estelle, I don't think the birds outside heard you properly." Sarcasm isn't a colour Ainsley uses often, but it was necessary there.

Estelle covers her mouth with a sheepish smile, but doesn't apologise.

"How? When? Last time we spoke we were trying to get her out of this festival so you wouldn't have to deal with any complications." Estelle puts down her carving tool and the candle she had been inscribing for the glamouring ritual to be placed in the house, too engrossed in the conversation now.

And, to be honest, Ainsley herself cannot believe it either. Yet for the past week, she kept circling back around to Priscilla — over breakfast, lunch, dinner… Bed. All she could think of while she took her morning walks through the woods, as she traversed vista after vista, things she had never given a second thought before. All she could think of was how she wanted to bring Priscilla to those places, to let her enjoy the beauty of this world with her by Ainsley's side.

Would she look at them with the same wonder she had so gracefully imparted onto her home, onto Ainsley then? Would she let herself wander?

Would she let Ainsley follow?

She hoped so.

But thoughts like these were inconsequential, however much Ainsley hoped they would come true.

"It does not matter, does it? I have made my mind clear about my situation, and that has not changed, Estelle. No matter how much I may wish for it to."

Besides, Priscilla did not deserve another burden placed on her shoulders. She had told her very little about herself so far — that she had moved from a different country, that she loved vintage furniture and fashions, but the way she avoided any talks of a family of blood and always defaulted to her best friend's instead spoke worlds about a sore spot she'd rather not touch.

Ainsley did not wish to add to her problems.

"After you left, I did exactly what I had told you I would — I talked to her. I came into the conversation expecting to swiftly turn her down after a few exchanged sentences, but..."

"Go on." Estelle encourages.

"I am not sure. I caught her in a daze — she looked at this place with such respect. She was warm and friendly even when I pointed out a glaring flaw in her work. We sat for tea as I explained all the intricacies of the festival, the history behind it." Ainsley hums in thought. Priscilla didn't just listen to her for the sake of her job.

She cared.

Estelle leans back in her seat, a smug grin on her face. Her legs are crossed and she swings a foot with the excitement of being correct.

"Hah! Look at you two lovebirds. She's interested too."

"Impossible." Ainsley jumps to dismiss it with a wave of the arm, but she barely believes her own words.

"Oh, for someone who's lived for so long and is supposed to be oh so wise — You really can't catch a hint if it hits you in the eye." Estelle points a candle in Ainsley's direction. "Why don't you just ask her then, darling? I know, I know, you think it'd be a huge mistake or whatever. But that's not your choice to make now, is it? Let her have a say. What's the harm?"

All of it, that's what, Ainsley thinks. Especially because she knows...

If Priscilla asks, Ainsley does not think she will be strong enough to deny her.

❧

Priscilla waves to Orion as his car makes its way back down the mountain.

She makes her way through the thick foliage of the narrow path to the mansion, and the sweet aroma of the front garden hits her before she gets there. But that's not all — as she finally can see her destination the smell of burnt diesel mixes with it.

A lorry is parked just to the side of the estate. A group of uniforms works hard unloading solid mahogany chairs and moving them into the mansion's wide open front doors.

Priscilla is so confused. For the very early shipment of the seats they will need, yes, but also — she looks around the thick walls of trees all around. Did she really miss a path big enough for something of that size? Orion could have been dropping her off so much closer all this time.

But no matter how hard she looks, all she can see is the way where she came in.

She shakes her head and chuckles. Another one to the list of mysteries surrounding these woods.

She skirts around two workers already bringing one of the round tables inside. There, she spots Estelle showing them to a room where they can store the furniture for the time being. Supervising the ordeal, Ainsley talks to a man who is, somehow, even taller than her — Priscilla is almost sure he had to duck to make his way through most doors, everywhere. He's of powerful build and uses the same branded black t-shirt and jeans as the rest of his team.

"How can I ever repay this most generous gesture, Zack?" Ainsley asks him, following the coming and going of it with her gaze.

"Don't mention it, ma'am, boss was chuffed to hear you were back. Least he wanted to do was help out if he could. Hell, he might be more excited than my kids for this party of yours." He adjusts the tip of his cap and shifts his weight to his other leg. "Which reminds me, the missus sends her regards. Hopes you have an easier time on your next h—"

"Priscilla." Her eyes catch up with the door and Ainsley interrupts him as she approaches.

Her usually calm and poised demeanour has changed, she notices. There's the edge of whatever secret she was trying to keep there, yes, Zack's expression conveying the same as his lips shut. But Ainsley's is different — yet Priscilla cannot quite place it.

"This is Zack Hogg, a good friend of mine. He's here on behalf of Mr. Millers, another good friend who was so kind to lend us the chosen furniture at no cost. Zack, this is Priscilla Cardoso, our decorator for the festival."

Priscilla scurries her mind. Millers, Millers… She has heard that name before.

It finally clicks.

"Millers… Of Miller's Treasures?" She has passed that store hundreds of times, longingly admiring their items on display, but never daring to enter. Interior, exterior, custom-made, antiques. They sell the good stuff. One-of-a-kinds.

"A pleasure, ma'am." He extends a hand to Priscilla who takes it excitedly.

"The pleasure is all mine! Please send my thanks to Mr. Miller as well — gosh, his items are impeccable. I can't believe I get to work with them."

He nods to her, and then to Ainsley. "I should pull my weight now and help with the unloading. I'll be back tomorrow with the rest." And he leaves, but not before almost imparting a courteous bow towards Ainsley. He remembers Priscilla's presence, however, and merely tips his hat again.

"Are we expecting even more to arrive?" Priscilla asks.

Ainsley nods. "Some of my guests have different… sitting needs." Between others. Zack isn't even the tallest of the orcs who were invited. "They're adjusting the items for them as we speak."

"Oh, of course." This wouldn't be the first venue Priscilla would help make accessible. "Let me know if I can make any other adjustments to the space. I know who to call if we need a temporary ramp for the entrance stairs."

Ainsley smiles warmly but shakes her head. "Estelle and I are already on the task, but I appreciate the offer." She may be able to explain the different chairs for the orcs and goblins, but other adjustments might be a tad trickier.

With that conversation sorted, they stare at each other in silence as they each wait for the other to say something.

Priscilla is the one to break it.

"You look very nice today. I love the new accessories." She compliments her, but the one that gets flustered is Priscilla.

"Ah, yes." Ainsley, suddenly conscious of her appearance, brings a hand to her ear where a pendant now hangs from her left side only. "Thank you."

This gives her a stealthy reason to double-check the glamour-infused earring she had been gifted by Estelle — a single golden teardrop on her left side, the magic working as a redundancy system since the entire premise of her house had been warded and spelled earlier. Convenient in case she needed to leave, nonetheless. She touches it then, and the item is strangely cold despite being worn for hours. A material symbol of one of the bridges keeping her and Priscilla's worlds apart.

Human trust in magic has always been variable — she remembers periods of peace and war alike. Lifetime friends and eternal foes. For the past few centuries, they have relied heavily upon machine and science. Ainsley is one of the few with the perspective to realise they simply developed 'magic' of their own — a different process, the same earth and sky fuelling it as any spell.

How close is the gap, how easily she could simply hop from one side to the other.

Yet there they stand, five centimetres and a thousand miles of a paradox apart.

"Oh! Don't move." Priscilla's excited voice rings, and she fights her instinct to jump.

Ainsley is positive she's reaching for the earring, fear almost carrying her then. But Priscilla simply rests her hand on Ainsley's shoulder.

She complies, standing still as she feels Priscilla's hand lie there right at the neckline of her dress. Her touch is soft and warm, sending goosebumps down Ainsley's spine. Priscilla is closer than she's ever been, and Ainsley takes her time studying her features. Her long lashes, her eyes squinting, and the way she bites her lower lip in concentration.

It lasts a second, or perhaps an eternity that she doesn't wish to end before Priscilla reveals what she had held her breath for.

On her index finger, small, red and winged — a ladybug.

Priscilla smiles, slowly turning her hand to keep up with the creature's trajectory around her arm.

"They're a sign of good luck, you know? A good omen, if you believe in such things."

More than ever, she does.

"Poor thing, it must be tired." Priscilla wastes no time, and just as easily she had hopped to its aid, she does to its comfort.

She takes her time placing her hand on the birch's trunk, and just… waits, until the bug is safely trailing its way up as if nothing had happened.

And she feels it, Priscilla's touch on her literal and figurative soul as her warmth spreads over Ainsley.

"I should get started now." Priscilla excuses herself, unaware of the weight of her last steps. Unaware of the impact she had just imparted onto Ainsley.

Unaware she was the one to take the leap.

The tables might be sorted, but this is a spring festival. It's definitely too early for any flowers to be delivered, but they will need some sort of structure to lie on.

Today, she brought some extra-strength rope and she has put it everywhere she could — wrapped around the many pillars that sit between halls and the inner patio, draped at the intersection between lower and upper floor — knotting it securely around the rails of the second floor alone took the good portion of an hour.

And it would have taken infinitely longer had Ainsley not been there to help her. Especially when tying the sections that would go from one side of the roof to the other for the colourful flags — being over six feet has its perks.

It's hard work, and it takes all afternoon as she had predicted. But through all of this, she catches Ainsley stealing looks, only to quickly look away when caught. Her hands lingering for a moment longer than needed when being handed the rope. A hand on the small of Priscilla's back as they cross paths in their dance to reach difficult places.

She wouldn't mind if more of her days were filled with this silent closeness. But she wants more too.

"What next?" Ainsley asks as she tiptoes to hook the last section of rope on the top of the wooden rail pillar.

Priscilla has the other end of it and gathers its bulk in a neat bundle so they can wait for the decorations and finish tying it then.

She takes a deep breath. The filtered sunlight hits them just as it peeks from a cloud. This is her chance.

"Now… I ask for your number." Priscilla can feel her heartbeat in her ears, her voice barely over a whisper.

Ainsley stops in her tracks, and she lets the rope fall to the floor before finishing tying it, but she doesn't dare face Priscilla. She stiffens, holding her hands on her back as if keeping a posture would protect her.

"I'm not sure that would be wise."

Priscilla's smile falters, but she can't believe all those stolen looks meant nothing. Something is keeping her. She takes a step closer, resting her hands on the railing so they can both look at the filtered light coming in over the roof.

"Why not?" She asks.

"Because… There are things about me, things you don't know, Priscilla. Things that would make this — that would make *us* — Difficult." If not downright impossible. Her lips press, trying to keep down her nerves.

This sounds more serious than a simple move for business. But instead of pressing her for answers, Priscilla opens up as well.

"I get it. There's plenty about myself that isn't as pretty as my face, you know?" She gives Ainsley a nervous laugh. "It took me a long time to even find out who that person was in the first place. And then an even longer time to learn to love the ugly truths about myself. Soul, mind and body."

Ainsley finally dares to look at her. Priscilla's face is serene, so sure of the peace in this truth that she has found that Ainsley wants to believe it too.

"I'm not saying I'm there yet. I don't think anyone can be. But I don't think it's about being perfect like that, for yourself or anyone else. I think…"

She meets her gaze, and Priscilla's eyes glisten with honesty.

"I just want the journey with you. For however long you can have me."

Ainsley stands there, motionless. She doesn't know what to think.

Who is this woman in front of her? Where has she been all these years?

How can she be so… sure?

Deep in thought, the moment passes, and Priscilla assumes it's her hint to leave.

"I understand your decision, though." She takes a slow step back. "And I won't bother you about it either. Next time I'm here, it will be just for work." Priscilla nods solemnly, sealing the deal, and expects any sort of acknowledgement from Ainsley.

But she is still far away in thought, her eyes unfocused on the tree, brows furrowed, hands held and clenched.

'Why? Why bring me back one last time, just to suffer?' She pleads in silent prayer to her heart. 'To make *her* suffer? Answer me.'

It's futile — for she knows her heart is with her now and not in the tree, and she was already told what it wants.

She's almost too late.

Priscilla affords herself a bitter, silent laugh amidst the hurt, being on the receiving end of an unresponsive daydreamer. Oh, the irony.

She has turned to leave, then, with no words left to say and her peace made. She takes her phone out to type a quick text for Orion to pick her up, and to grab that tub of ice cream on his way there. She almost sends it.

"Wait."

She stops and turns. Ainsley closes the distance between them and reaches into one of the pockets of her long dress.

She produces a small piece of notebook paper, folded over in anxiety so many times the creases are a permanent part of it now. Inscribed on it, however, is a phone number.

Ainsley's phone number.

Priscilla takes it in her hand, and she looks up to Ainsley with that sparkle.

"How long?…"

"Since the night after I met you."

Priscilla's eyes widen. Ainsley steps closer, close enough for Priscilla to feel her breath and smell the wild berries of her hair.

Ainsley takes Priscilla's hand, placing the note on her palm and closing it.

"It is a landline number, however. You will have to call." Estelle had brought her up to date on most of the technology she missed, but the intricacies of the internet still elude her.

Priscilla answers with an incredulous laughter, shaking her head.

"You're truly a one-of-a-kind woman, Ainsley."

She hums in agreement, and brings a hand up to Priscilla's face, tracing a line on the soft curve of her jaw to her chin.

"Likewise."

Goosebumps rise on Priscilla's skin. Eyes half-lidded, she loses herself in the feeling of Ainsley's calloused fingertips on her face, her floral fragrance mixing with Priscilla's perfume.

But she has enough sense left to steady herself on Ainsley's waist and reach for her lips with her own.

It's a sweet thing at first. She tastes of cardamom and her skin feels so warm, almost too warm, and present. Her hair is inviting as she slides a hand on Ainsley's neck, pulling them even closer together as if physicality is both a reason and an afterthought.

They explore each other, learning the intricacies of the other's breath, and only stopping when they're almost out of their own.

"So... What's next?" Priscilla asks, short of breath, mimicking the exact question made at her that started all this.

Ainsley takes Priscilla's free hand in hers.

"Walk with me?"

# Chapter 5

It's a warm day, too warm for spring, however close to summer it is. Priscilla feels it, being so unaccustomed to hiking, especially as the light starts fading into a sunset. She's glad she dressed light today, loose jeans shorts and a button-up t-shirt, expecting the hard work of that afternoon to wear her out in office clothes.

Ainsley feels it too, even more so. She is used to the walks in the forest, but her discomfort did not start now. It's why she woke up today and dressed in only a simple cotton dress with a belt, feeling the heat before she even stepped outside.

It is just too warm, unnaturally so. Every plant and animal in this forest can feel it too, and her connection to it only worsens the sensation.

Which makes the location Ainsley is taking them to all the more perfect.

Priscilla is glad the way isn't too steep, but she feels like she should be struggling more with the path. And realistically, she should. But Ainsley guides her to more secure footing, more even ground, knowing every bend of this land and teaching Priscilla how to traverse it.

"We have only a few more minutes ahead. You are doing quite well for someone who claims they have no experience hiking." Ainsley says as she takes Priscilla's hand to help her up a steep incline.

"Only because you're here." She struggles up but makes it nonetheless, patting her clothes before they continue.

"I beg to differ. I can only do so much — you are the one to put in the effort."

But Priscilla doesn't register the comment. As she looks up from her clothes to the way ahead, her breath is taken by the vista that greets her at the top of that battle uphill.

The trees open to a vast meadow. Grass, shrubs and flowers galore compete for the delight of adorning their evening in this hike. Small clusters of oaks and other trees are scattered near the bottom, where it all merges into the mountains up ahead, their peaks still slightly powdered by snow. To their side, in the distance, Priscilla can see the city start to light up for the night.

"Whoa…" That is all she can say. "You're really telling me we aren't there yet? This is incredible!"

"It is. One of many oases hidden away in this forest, yet no less beautiful for it." Ainsley chuckles. "We may settle here if you'd rather."

If this isn't the destination, then what a journey. Priscilla can't even imagine what is waiting for her wherever Ainsley plans to take them. Perhaps another time, when there's more sunlight to appreciate all this. For now?

"I have a better idea." Priscilla shakes her head, letting her smile turn a bit devious.

She taps Ainsley on her shoulder and immediately bolts downhill, leaving Ainsley behind with their picnic basket in hand, and struggling to run without knowing the levels of the ground below her amidst all the fully bloomed wildflowers.

"Last one has to set down dinner!" Priscilla sets the terms with a massive head start already underway, her voice diluted by the distance.

Ainsley, still taken by surprise, lets out a loud laugh at the sheer confidence Priscilla has just displayed by such a challenge. She takes her time making sure their food is safely fastened inside the basket before letting gravity pull her steps down as she runs to catch up.

Which she does, fast, unimaginably so. Even if you do not count her lifetimes' worth of experience threading her way around this forest, her legs are much longer than any human's and most magical folk's — including Priscilla's.

She would have surpassed Priscilla easily too, if she wanted to. But as their paths cross, Ainsley can only see the joy in her face as she giggles and giggles, extending a hand to Ainsley so she may join in.

And, just like that, any trace of competition dissolves from both their minds.

With their hands connected, they pick up speed. Even with Ainsley's guidance now, it proves too much, their steps out of sync as they trip and tumble into each other. Ainsley is fast enough to let the picnic basket go as Priscilla hugs her and they roll down the few remaining feet of the slope, gravity taking over.

They land safely at the bottom, still enwrapped together, neither managing to contain their unfiltered emotions that reverberate in this open meadow.

Their night has barely started, but for now, they are content to just look into each other's eyes and appreciate this simple joy of a frolic amongst a flowered meadow.

They reach what seems to be a fork in their path. By then, it's almost completely dark, the last rays of silver and purple the only memory of the sun.

Thankfully their adventure earlier had not ruined their food — not that it matters. At this point, food is the last thing in their minds.

"How can you see anything anymore?" Priscilla asks, squinting to even make out the silhouette of Ainsley.

"I cannot." She states plainly. " This forest is my home as much as the mansion is, if not more now. I've been wandering these woods in the dark for as long as I have in the light. At some point you just learn to feel your way around, trust your other senses and your instincts and you simply… Become part of it."

Priscilla laughs, not at Ainsley — but at how her words would validate so many of Orion's fears about Ainsley's origins.

"What is so amusing about that?" Ainsley asks in earnest, if a tad curious.

"Nothing, it's silly. What you said just reminded me — My best friend, Orion? He has some stories… He thinks you used to be a man that lived in your mansion twenty years ago, who disappeared mysteriously." She laughs. "Get this, he believes you're some sort of ghost."

Ainsley stiffens, her hand tightening around Priscilla's.

A ghost is not the same as what Ainsley is, but it's incredibly close to the truth.

"Do you?"

Priscilla shakes her head, getting closer to her.

"A ghost? Hm-hm, no. Especially not after that kiss."

But she doesn't voice that vision of Ainsley she had on that first day. That one, she yearned to believe in.

Now she has the real one right in front of her, and she couldn't have asked for more.

Ainsley gives her another kiss then, much faster now but just as sweet, before grabbing her by the waist and submerging both in the thick foliage in between the forked paths in front of them.

Priscilla yelps, but Ainsley protects her from most branches and vines that try to tangle them up. A moment later, they resurface, and Priscilla has to wait for her eyes to adjust to the new lights.

A grove, embedded into the walls of the mountain, and a waterfall that cascades down to form a pool. Weeping willow trees seclude this corner of the forest, and tiny little specks of fireflies, alive and in song, paint the inviting water's reflection.

"Ainsley… This is gorgeous!" Priscilla cannot stop staring at it all, her eyes reflecting just as many fireflies as the water in front of her.

That this place has been hiding away… She cannot believe how lucky she is to experience it. To be here, with Ainsley.

"Yes… " But Ainsley's gaze does not leave Priscilla's. To her, this oasis pales in comparison to the woman who explores it.

Ainsley lets her wander and dream then, and she gladly accepts the invitation. This abundant with water, shielded from the sun all day, the breeze that hits them offers much-needed relief from the weather. Priscilla looks up, the first stars of the night and their older sister, Venus, greeting her with their light.

She reaches the edge of the pool and promptly takes her shoes off, placing them on a rock nearby. The contact of her feet with the water is shocking at first, but the temperature levels eventually and all that is left is bliss as she sits down.

A night under the stars with Ainsley — it sounds too good to be true. For once in her life, the real cannot compare to fantasy.

"As nice as dinner by the lake sounds at the moment —" Ainsley says as she catches up to Priscilla.

But instead of sitting by her side, she reaches the same rock Priscilla had chosen to put her shoes on. Ainsley's boots join them, and so do her socks, her belt, her dress — layer by layer is shed, until there's only Ainsley left.

Priscilla is tempted to look at the sky again. Not to avert her eyes, oh no. But to make sure Venus herself didn't descend from her place by the moon to grace the Earth with her presence tonight. As Ainsley sinks onto the water, Priscilla cannot help comparing her to the painting — and how unlike it, her long hair betrays any attempt of incidental cover as it trails and floats behind her.

Her skin is flush with colour and Priscilla doesn't have to wonder how far her freckles descend any more. They're there, on display; down her neck, shoulder, arms. Accenting her small breasts so beautifully. Her long locks of hair frame her dipped hips and Priscilla wonders how her hands would fit on their sides. She submerges in the water, and her hair clings to all the right places as she resurfaces brushing the water away from her face, eyes locked on Priscilla.

"Wouldn't you rather join me?"

Priscilla would love nothing more than to be there as well, to explore every surface of Ainsley's body and lose herself in it, but she hesitates as her thoughts drift to her own.

She's a goddess. You're not good enough to live up to what she deserves.

A borrowed thought once again, she acknowledges, and one that is hard to part with.

Ainsley can see her gears turning.

"Nothing more needs to happen tonight, Priscilla — not even a simple, innocent swim. I will avert my gaze if that would make you more comfortable, but I won't deny that I have been as infatuated by your figure as I have been by your actions."

The desire in her eyes is piercing and shakes Priscilla from her spiral. She stands up then, changing her seat to a half lean against one of those big rocks where their clothes lay, feet still submerged.

"Come help me?"

Ainsley smiles. "As you wish."

She closes the distance between them, placing herself comfortably between Priscilla's legs. The uneven footing has them almost at each other's eye level, face to face, only a breath away.

Ainsley begins with Priscilla's shirt — undoing the stylized knot at the bottom and up. Button by button, exposing her wide waist and soft stomach, her full breasts held by a lacy bralette. She lets the shirt fall back, slowly sliding it down Priscilla's shoulders and traces a languid line from neck to chest. Down, tugging on the lace on its way, and circling around to unclasp it, savouring every second in silence.

Priscilla stays immovable, losing herself in every sensation as Ainsley's careful touches spread over her, her breath hitching along the way.

"Your friend was wrong about many things, but he did have one piece of information he gathered correctly, even if by complete coincidence."

"Oh?" Priscilla manages to let out in between gasps. Her bra slides from her as well, falling to the side and exposing her chest to Ainsley's body heat, not yet touching but so close.

"I have always struggled with trying to place any labels on myself. Man, woman, none of it has ever quite fit, no matter how much I have stretched myself thin to try and understand it."

With how fast some of the signifiers of gender have changed throughout time, especially for a being that has lived for so long, it's hard to keep up. At some point, Ainsley had just decided it was more convenient to give up and embrace the figure she had come to find comfort in as it is.

"So, no, I have never been a man. But I cannot say for certain I have ever been a woman either, not fully. Certain appearances will call to me from time to time, but they are superficial still and in no way a clear reflection."

"Oh. I understand." Priscilla may not relate to Ainsley's experience, but she knows the pitfalls of performance — how suffocating it can be to try to achieve an ideal, never succeeding, always incentivised to. "But I can't say I see how this is relevant right now."

Ainsley places her hand around Priscilla's back, resting one of her calloused thumbs on the hem of Priscilla's jeans in preparation for the rest of her plans.

"Before we go any further, I thought you needed to know. In case it changed how you felt about me." She cannot bring herself to open up completely just yet — rules need to be followed. But she hoped this was enough for now.

Priscilla shakes her head.

"I'm glad you're trusting me with something so personal. But there's not a lot you can say for me to release my grip from you right now, Ainsley. Besides…"

She pictures what a more butch Ainsley would look like — short hair, perhaps, a linen vest over a neatly ironed shirt, tight slacks? Oh, this does nothing to stoke the fire building in her.

Priscilla hooks a finger around the golden, delicate neck chain Ainsley still wears to pull her closer. "I wouldn't mind seeing your other moods if they ever strike, especially if I can look at them from right here in this position."

A corner of Ainsley's mouth rises before crashing against Priscilla's. They are full of passion now, a push, a pull, strong hands everywhere yet not there yet. An eternity like this would pass too soon, both lost in each other's taste.

But Ainsley is nothing but more patient with her process of undressing Priscilla, almost irritatingly so. She takes her time unzipping the last layer, pulling the shorts down her legs while dotting kisses along her torso, each one sending shivers down Priscilla's neck.

"Ainsley…" She wraps her hand on Ainsley's hair as she descends.

"Yes?" She asks as if she doesn't know what she's doing.

"I don't think I can take any more teasing… If you don't do something, I will." Her breath is laboured and her back arches against the stone.

"Patience." Ainsley displays unlikely strength for her stature, picking up Priscilla and adjusting her higher on the rock without any struggle. "This is as much torture for me as it is for you, but tonight I intend to worship your body, Priscilla. I am not leaving until I have explored every centimetre of you. Until I have stolen every single breath. Until you are completely satisfied. After that you are free to do to me whatever your heart desires, and then some. Tonight, I'm yours."

Priscilla inhales deeply, almost overwhelmed by that promise but never taking her eyes away from the recipient of her affections.

"Will you let me?" She brings a hand to Priscilla's face, tracing her bottom lip, expectantly, her voice saying more than her words.

"Please, Ainsley. I'm yours too."

She hums, content, placing a hand on Priscilla's chest and pushing until her skin is flush against the stone under them. Ainsley resumes her descent again, peppering Priscilla's skin with even more kisses as she goes.

She places herself right over Priscilla's thighs, locking one of them with her arm for leverage, a hand ever caressing her waist. She stays there for a moment, entranced by the sight she finds.

And what a sight — her perfume mixing with her desire a powerful aphrodisiac. Ainsley's free hand begins exploring, up her thick inner thigh, over her narrow hips, and finally down to her drenched lips. A ghost touch. Up. Down. Spreading them open for her viewing.

Perfection. Priscilla is every wonder of this world and so much more.

"Ainsley…" She pleads again in a whisper, squirming, but she had been warned, and Ainsley's ministrations do not change.

The touches turn into her entire mouth, lavishing her in one long swipe of her tongue, stopping only to lazily paint circles at the top. A single digit of Ainsley's hand presses against her entrance, never making its way in, simply tracing its shape with intent.

She keeps her there, at this slow, torturous speed for what feels like the sweetest eternity — every so often breaking the barrier and giving her something for her walls to wrap around, only to take it away again.

While she's kept there, Ainsley's free hand caresses every surface of her body, leaving a trail of goosebumps wherever it touches. She meant her words, promising to explore her entirety and she takes her time with that too

— spending a good portion giving due attention to her breasts. Her touch is ever so soft as she circles her hardened nipples repeatedly.

Every moan Priscilla gladly gives Ainsley she promptly archives in her memory, drawing a mental map of what brings her the most response — those sounds are the only thing breaking the constant noise of the water and the singing of the crickets around them. She uses this new arsenal to bring Priscilla up, lavishing her body with her mouth — just to leave her hanging at the top, stopping to take another good look at the woman under her and deriving her own pleasure from the sights she sees there.

Rinse, repeat, until Priscilla's words are an incoherent mess in between her pleads.

"Ainsley… Ainsley, please, I —"

It doesn't take much more to bring her over the edge. Absolutely lost in the constant trickling stream of sensations, all it takes is a single droplet in an already overflowing cup to break her — a flick of her tongue as she buries her fingers into Priscilla, and she comes undone.

Her thighs treble as Ainsley keeps them in place, and the storm of pleasure takes over her body. She's completely spent as she slowly comes down, breathing heavily as Ainsley decides she's satisfied with her work for now.

She comes up for a kiss and Priscilla can taste herself in her breath, musk mixed with Ainsley's sweetness. Ainsley stays there over her, cradling her face until she's coherent enough to open her eyes and form a sentence with her laboured breathing.

" — Oh, Ainsley, I… I don't have the words. Where did you learn all that?" Her smile is pure bliss.

Ainsley cannot contain the melodic laugh that she lets out as she lazily traces Priscilla's jaw.

"I would like to believe my years have given me some experience in this field. Seems I have enough accumulated skill to leave you satisfied — however longer I still wish to keep exploring your body."

Priscilla's eyes widen.

"You want to give me another round?"

Ainsley throws a leg over Priscilla, straddling her and pinning her down. Her hands by the sides of Priscilla's head support her, and her now partially dry hair curtains the perfect framing of the night sky against her face.

"I have barely scratched the surface, Priscilla."

She's almost tempted to let her do it, then, her want rising again momentarily. But as her eyes feast on Ainsley's figure over her, she sees the state she has left Ainsley in as her fluids drip down her thigh, glistening under the low light of this grove.

Her thoughts travel somewhere else.

"You promised me I could do anything I wanted to you after you were done with me," Priscilla says, her words barely registering back as her hands rise from her sides to tentatively explore Ainsley's chest. She brushes them with her fingertips and Ainsley takes a deep breath, closing her eyes to savour those sensations.

"Are you satisfied already?" She opens them again to look at Priscilla with her hungry gaze, slowly grinding her hips over her as Priscilla's hands don't stop there. They travel down to where their legs meet, welcomed by Ainsley's overwhelming desire as she slides a finger in between her lips.

She feels divine in her warmth, and the sounds that escape her mouth are a hymn to the heavens in that melodic voice. Ainsley throws her head back, her hips moving back and forth with intent now, chasing Priscilla's touch on her.

"I won't be satisfied until I find out what you taste like. Come here —"

Priscilla gives in to that earlier thought and grabs her by the dip of her hips, confirming her theory as soon as they make contact — her hands were made to be placed there at Ainsley's sides, her pull guiding her up with hunger.

Ainsley almost loses her balance on top of that rock as she is shifted on her knees to hover over Priscilla's head, legs spread, sitting absolutely exposed a mere centimetre away from her face.

"Priscilla — Ah…"

Whatever Ainsley was going to say gets cut off as Priscilla takes her first taste of Ainsley, and oh how sweet she is. Priscilla drinks freely, her hands firm on Ainsley's hip to keep her steady over her as her mouth explores every surface she's afforded.

"Oh, Priscilla. Don't stop." She exhales, already so worked up from earlier that even the smallest touch unravels her.

Priscilla feels it in the way she fails miserably to stay still, struggling under her grip as she picks up her pace to match Ainsley's. In a few seconds, their rhythms sync, and Priscilla feels Ainsley's legs tremble over her. Ainsley grips Priscilla's legs behind her, trying to steady herself as she moans into the night.

It doesn't take much more for her to come undone right now, right there — just Priscilla's tongue exploring

a bit further. She buries it inside of her, curving it up with intent and Ainsley stills over Priscilla as she clenches around her in her release. Priscilla drinks every sweet drop as Ainsley melts on top of her, savouring the high in her laboured breath before collapsing by Priscilla's side.

Priscilla wipes the corner of her mouth, any lipstick she had on long gone now. She holds Ainsley close, looking deep into her half-lidded eyes as she comes down.

"Now… Are you satisfied?" Ainsley asks in between long breaths, a lazy smile painted on her face.

Priscilla chuckles. "As long as you are."

"Physically? Yes." Ainsley hums in thought, their faces so close to each other as they lie together on that rock." Yet I feel there's still so much left to uncover on what makes you give me such delectable noises, Priscilla. So many spots on your divine body still begging my touch."

Priscilla can feel her desire rise again as she considers the offer, however soon her logical mind and tired body complain it to be. But a sudden interruption comes from her own betraying body as her stomach lets out a long cry for dinner.

She stills, embarrassed, but all Ainsley does is let out a lighthearted laugh before getting up.

"It can wait — we both could do with some food right now."

Ainsley offers her a hand, and they both make their leisurely way to one of the weeping willows, without bothering to dress up again. They find a nice spot under its canopy to place down their picnic cloth, and Ainsley insists on being the one to set their food — announcing herself the official loser of their earlier game, despite Priscilla's complaints.

Soon, they're surrounded by delicious dishes — sandwiches, biscuits, pies, scones, tarts. A wide selection that they will never finish tonight. But they feast, taking turns to offer the other something they have not tried yet — Priscilla learns that Ainsley is a vegetarian and Ainsley comes to the conclusion Priscilla hates eggs, despite her excuses.

They enjoy their full bellies almost as much as they enjoy this quiet intimate moment — Priscilla lays her head on Ainsley's chest as she gently caresses her hair, and they both look up to the sky.

"What occupies your mind?" Ainsley asks, noticing Priscilla's gaze darting from one star to the other.

"You. Us. The universe."

"A tad late at night to ponder the intricacies of existence, is it not?" Ainsley asks but her smile does not falter.

Priscilla snuggles up closer.

"It's no use, it happens every time I look up at the stars. All of this vast emptiness just makes me think about my place in it, you know?"

Ainsley does, too closely. Once, she did not need to look up. Once, it was all so simple. Yet lately the void has become somewhat of a close acquaintance.

"I understand. It truly puts things in perspective."

Priscilla nods, but their minds could not be different at that moment.

"Aren't we just so lucky?"

"…Lucky?" Ainsley raises an eyebrow.

"Well, yeah. Out of the possibilities, all of the places in space and time, I was lucky to exist now. Not in Palaeolithic times, or ancient China, or Victorian England, or even the future somewhere in, I don't know, Jupiter — whatever that will look like." She chuckles. "Here. Now."

She looks to Ainsley, and her earnest spark is there again, so hopeful, so close.

"To sleep in on Sundays because we stayed up late binge-watching a new period drama while we ate pizza. To wake up to a beautiful sunrise and be late for work. To think you've had the worst year of your life to wake up a year later for that to feel so distant. To just… Share the gift of life with so many others. For them to share it with you."

"For another wonderful night under the stars with you, Ainsley. If that makes me a tiny speck on the grand design of things —" She makes a great gesture. "Then I'll be a happy speck, glad to know I did my part."

Ainsley cannot find the words, but Priscilla does not ask for any. She simply parts another kiss on her lips, a quick thing that sears its mark in Ainsley's conscience.

She has no time to process — no, she doesn't wish to. Not here, not now.

Right now, she chooses to be present. To feel her there as she takes her side of the bargain and so earnestly gives back.

Their hips lock now, swaying back and forth, a leg over a shoulder. They lose track of where one ends and the other begins as they feed each other chocolate-covered strawberries and forget to count how many times they come that night. It's too much and not enough. So real. So needed.

Two specks, becoming one.

# Chapter 6

"Knock knock, we're here! Ainsley!" Estelle calls out as soon as she's through the door.

Time is running short and the more critical parts of the festival need to be set in motion. That is why today Estelle brings all three generations of the Nowaks to location — grandmother, father and daughter, all skilled bakers and cooks in their own right.

But Ainsley isn't in to greet them.

"Set up shop in the kitchen and get yourselves comfortable." Estelle instructs. "She's probably just in the back, I'll get her."

Estelle's hunch is correct. Ainsley stands amidst her garden, a light dungaree over a white shirt, bunched up at the elbows and a comically big straw hat on her head, she idly waters her crops under the scalding sun. But Estelle doesn't find her alone.

"Tommy! What are you doing here!?" She's shocked to find her son scurrying around the plants in wolf form, gnawing at a particularly hard stem.

"He's being a very kind young wolf by helping me tend the garden," Ainsley answers the question for him as he's too preoccupied with destroying a particular weedling before it overtakes the entire plot, but he takes a second to breathe and bark in his mother's direction with pride.

"Ian asked if I would be so kind as to babysit for an hour or two. Something about some time alone with your oldest. It seemed quite pressing."

"Ah, that. Mae is struggling quite a bit with her wolf side lately, so Ian told me he wanted to take her on a one-on-one lesson, but I never thought it would be so soon." Estelle explains with a sigh.

"I am sorry to hear that. But you don't seem as nervous about this as Ian was." Ainsley notes.

"Oh, you remember me back then, all the trouble I stirred in my coven. This is just like that, it's just something every witch needs to go through at that age. Find their own voice and whatnot. I gave what wisdom I could give and he's going the extra five miles — but the rest Mae will have to figure out alone."

Ainsley hums. "What a fortunate child, to have such caring parents. You, against all odds, turned out to be a very good mother, Estelle."

She raises an eyebrow, but they both laugh nonetheless.

"Thank you for taking care of Tommy. I'll take him back home once we're done."

"Anytime, Estelle. He can be quite agreeable when he's chewing the right plants and not my tomato sprouts."

If Tommy hears it, he does not acknowledge the comment — instead parading around a particularly big stick he found on the ground.

"By the way—" She pushes Ainsley to the side, quickly casting a sound bubble around them for some privacy. "A wee birdie told me you took a certain someone to a certain grove in the forest for a picnic."

Oh, witches and their divination powers. It is involuntary, Ainsley concedes, but still quite annoying to be on its receiving end.

"This small bird would be correct. After you left that Thursday, we talked for a while — one thing led to the other, and, well…"

"Well?"

"I am not of the sort to kiss and tell, now am I?" Ainsley crosses her arms.

"She blew your back out, huh?" Her grin is devious.

"Estelle!"

She bellows out a laugh, throwing her head back, and Ainsley adjusts her pose to recentre herself after the display of such foul language — however true it was.

"Whatever she did, darling, she did a good job. You look lighter, like you let go of something that was weighing you down. You're completely different from that Ainsley that visited me that first week of May."

Ainsley agrees silently. She feels lighter too, ever since that night, and every call Priscilla has made to her ever since has been slowly chipping away at the rest of her anxiety.

"Alright, alright, as much as I'd love to listen to every juicy detail right now, catering is waiting for you, Ainsley. I'd get there ASAP if you don't want your entire kitchen transmuted."

"The Nowaks?" She asks.

"Who else?"

She leaves Estelle behind to deal with a now-human Tommy covered in dirt to meet some more of her old friends.

The Nowak family comes from a thriving fae line, widespread in politics ever since the rise of society itself. A small branch of it, however, grew tired of the backstabbing intricacies of such life and broke off to find a different calling.

Ainsley welcomed them with open hands then, and to this day their bakery is one of the few places she makes an effort to visit every time she comes down from the forest.

"Careful, young lady, that is a cast-iron skillet you are holding," Ainsley warns in jest as she enters her kitchen, knowing fully well that the lore behind the metal is nothing but a myth. She takes her hat off to duck under the door.

"Ainsley!" The two oldest sound off in unison.

"Hanna, Edmund." She greets them with a smile and a hug. "Ah, it has been too long."

"Yes, and whose fault was that, hm?" Hanna, the grandmother, asks. "But let bygones be bygones. It is good to see you again."

"Likewise. And how are you, Edmund?"

"Busy." He offers a tired smile. "Amanda is taking over the bakery so we've both been up and about in the wee hours of the day for weeks for her training."

He tilts his head to the young woman with the cast pan in her hands as she leaves it on the counter. She's the spitting image of her father, with long blonde hair tied to the side and permanently arched inner brows, but the iridescent wings on her back are an exact copy of her late grandfather's — may his soul rest in peace.

"Amanda, was it? Oh, you were barely five last I saw you, you must not even remember me — but how beautifully you've grown." Ainsley offers her a handshake instead, which she takes enthusiastically.

"I do, though! You used to make all the flowers on the porch grow really fast." She describes her memories with a fond smile. "It's very nice to meet you again, and I'm looking forward to the festival."

"This is her first big event as head of the bakery. I'll be supervising everything, but she will be the one calling the shots." Edmund explains.

"I promise not to disappoint!" She says, voice cracking with nervousness.

Ainsley holds both her hands to calm her down.

"You would never disappoint me, not even if you tried to. I look forward to working with you, Amanda."

She gives an enthusiastic nod before they're interrupted by the kitchen's telephone.

Ainsley excuses herself to answer it. She is not expecting any calls, with Priscilla bound to show up soon, so she picks it up with curiosity as the Nowaks resume their work.

"Hello?"

"Hello! Would Mr. Ainsley McBush be available to speak?"

Ainsley needs to pause to silently snicker at the surname. With no need for a family denominator, she has given many an 'interesting' last name throughout the years

— McBush being not even close to the wildest she would come up with.

"You are speaking to him. Who is this?"

"Mr. McBush, this is James Peterson from Hilltop Real Estate."

Ainsley's demeanour changes instantly. She remembers the unopened letter, now long discarded, and knows exactly where this phone call is going.

"We at Hilltop have an exclusive offer we would like to discuss with you. Would now be a good moment?"

"No, it would not. As a matter of fact, I will save us both this waste of time and ask that you do not bother me with any of this nonsense again. This land is not for sale, and this is final. Good day to you, Mr. Peterson."

She bangs her phone against its base on the wall and is visibly shaken. Sure, a phone call is nothing to avoid, but she has seen this happen too many times now. It never ends with *just* a phone call. She has a feeling she will be talking to this James fellow again.

"Everything alright, Ainsley?" Hanna is the one to ask.

She sighs, calming herself. She won't let this small incident ruin her mood, especially when she is among such precious friends.

"Yes, just some real estate company and their same old game. Nothing to worry about." She explains.

"Don't tell me — Hilltop?" Edmund asks.

"Yes, that is exactly who. How did you know?" Ainsley is concerned. Edmund crosses his arms.

"They've been pestering old Willy for months now. There's some big plans for a dam or such so they've been scoping for locations. At least that's what I've heard from his son."

"A dam?" Willy lives nearly on the other side of town, closer to the sea. What is the size of this 'opportunity' Hilltop is so eager to see come to fruition?

It matters not — Ainsley will not yield. She has been protecting this forest for as long as she could from memories, and she will continue to do so until...

Until she fades completely.

Once, she would let this thought flood her conscience, let it take reign in her mind. Now, she stands in a room full of those she cares for, preparing to host even more in these walls.

Even if she does fade, even if her tree decides it has tired of the walking world — they shall persist. Generations of people who may not roam the woods like they once did, but that she hopes still care for their roots.

And if Fate graces her with one more year amongst them, she won't take a single second for granted.

"Ainsley, don't get caught up, darling. Priscilla will be here soon." Estelle appears at the door, a squirming Tommy in her hands.

"Of course. Thank you, Estelle." She gives a warm smile and addresses the Nowaks. "You might wish to take a small break to enjoy the show. I do not put on this kind of performance very often."

"Oh! Summer of '83." Hanna exclaims, leaving her granddaughter confused.

"Precisely."

She directs all of them outside, back to the patio. The birch has never been this brightly in bloom in a long time —

petals falling and dotting the soft earth below. Ainsley walks to it as the others make themselves comfortable around her.

She places a soft touch against the bark, feeling the magic of her own soul resonate with her body. The taste of static fills the air as she connects with the Earth, not commanding but melding her will with its own. An unnatural wind sweeps all the petals in the ground as they circle Ainsley, her vines lifting with it in uncontrollable waves.

Her friends stiffen as they feel this surge in magic in their bones, the hairs on their necks rising with an eerie tingle — even little Tommy stays uncharacteristically still.

She turns, and from her steps, the ground blooms. All around her, it unfolds — flowers upon flowers sprouting from the ground, growing out of thin air. It spreads from there, grabbing onto the hempen rope she had installed with Priscilla and holding on for dear life. It climbs — around the pillars, spreading on the halls of the second floor as it overtakes the roof, clinging to the flags up top and curtaining down.

Every surface, every crevice — from the floor to the small space between wall and ceiling — is covered with budding flora, ready to fully bloom by their May Day.

"Wow…" Amanda untangles a piece of ivy that had clung to her shoulder on the spot of the wall she was leaning against. "I've never seen something like that."

"This is better than '83. Oh, people will love it, Ainsley." Hanna carefully steps around, taking everything in.

"No, no chewing on these, Tommy! Behave, darling." Estelle points a finger at him as she lets him out and joins Ainsley's side.

Her breathing is laboured after this great surge of magic, but otherwise, she's unfazed.

"I mean, what a show! Remind me never to get on your bad side." Estelle says.

Ainsley smiles.

"Do you think she will like it?" She adjusts her vines like a love-struck teenager as if she hadn't just raised a monument in Priscilla's name.

But Ainsley already knows she'll love it.

"We kinda just stayed like that, scissoring until my legs couldn't take the cramps any more and feeding each other sweets for dessert until the heat was too much and we wanted a proper soak in the lake…" Priscilla's mind is half there, half back at that wonderful night as she finishes recounting it to Orion.

They are parked just at the entrance of the narrow path to the mansion again, and Priscilla sways back and forth, hands clasped by her head as she dreamily overshares.

"I know! It looks like it's going so fast, but it has never felt this right… We've been calling every night since, just talking and watching Coronation Street together — She's taken me to the most beautiful parts of this forest too, things you wouldn't even be able to imagine, Orion! I think I might take her out this time, so I can show her some cool places too…"

"Aye, aye… Coronation Street… Scissoring…" He says mindlessly as he holds the steering wheel. "That's it—"

He jumps from his car, throwing the door wide open and making his way to the mansion.

"I'm walking in with ya and I'm placing a face to that goddamn name."

"What!?" Priscilla exclaims, getting out of the car as well, but she's being left behind as he makes a beeline to their destination through the trees.

"Did ya just want me to sit on my ass and expect we bump into each other in town? Fuck if that happens — Nah, I'm going in. Do you know if she has any friends? Single ones? Who live somewhere it doesn't take a fucking hike to get to?"

"Orion!" But she has accepted that nothing will stop him now.

She's not exactly angry at him for wanting to meet Ainsley — he's basically a brother to her, and she was going to do the whole 'meet the family' bit at some point.

But this is her last week working on this project, and Orion can be… Short with his words. She just hopes everything goes smoothly, and mixing him into the equation throws all her expectations off.

"Huh." He says when they emerge from the bushes. "This place is not as scary in spring. Go figure."

"When were you here before?" Priscilla asks.

"For that bet, remember? I stood right around here with the rest of those fools as my mate Rob went in. I'll tell ya, it's a different place when your arse is freezing."

He shrugs as Priscilla catches up, and they make their way to the front doors.

"Just… Try to keep the swearing down?"

"Right."

"And be prepared to look up."

"Got it." He blinks. "Holy shit —"

She sees it then, as Orion opens the doors to the patio.

Her senses are inundated by the smell of flowers — and they are everywhere. Primroses, bluebells, myrtles, daisies, orchids, violets — every conceivable surface around the birch tree is covered in perfect arrangements, swaying idly with the wind coming from outside.

As if her drawings had come to life.

"Priscilla—"

"Ainsley!"

There, amongst this vision directly from her dreams, Ainsley stands, arms wide open. Her hair is peppered in petals and her smile is as bright as the sun when she sees her.

Priscilla runs — past Orion, past the Nowaks, past Estelle and her son — meeting Ainsley amidst this fresh meadow and jumping into a tight kiss. They spin, once, twice with momentum, never letting go as they break the kiss so Priscilla can stand.

"This is… I, I can't even —" Priscilla is the one to be at a loss for words now. "Did you do all of this? By yourself?"

"I may have had some help from the… supplying florist. But I merely followed your plans, Priscilla. This is your achievement, your vision for the festival."

"Right, you just took the time and energy to actually arrange and put everything together to bring my vision to reality. No biggie." Priscilla rolls her eyes as best as she can with the happy tears falling from them.

"Precisely." Ainsley brings a hand to wipe them off.

If it were for them, they would stay there forever, holding each other until the petals have covered their love entirely. But their friends and family are there, delighted at the scene unfolding in silent but happy wishes for the couple, and Orion makes his presence known.

"I'll be damned, you were right Pri." He's talking about Ainsley's height, of course, but has enough tact to not mention it to her face.

"And who do I owe the pleasure of a visit?" Ainsley tenses for a millisecond as she hugs Priscilla tighter, the phone call too fresh in her mind as she looks out for stranger danger.

"Oh right, Ainsley — this is Orion Moore, my best friend." Priscilla is the one to introduce him, noticing Ainsley's defensiveness. "He insisted on meeting you, even if he was just dropping me off.

"Yo! Nice to put a face to the name." He extends a hand with a smug grin.

"It is nice to make your acquaintance as well, Mr. Moore." She takes his handshake firmly, having lowered her defences. "Priscilla has also recounted your many feats to me — and I thank you for taking such good care of her. You will always find a home in my house, as she has found in yours.

"You!" Amanda's voice is the one to surprisingly pierce through the introductions. Her already pinkish face reddens in anger as she recognises Orion.

"What the f— What are you doing here?" He asks, recognizing her as he looks past Ainsley.

"I'm catering for the festival, not that it's any of your business." She responds, pointing an accusatory finger at him.

"What is happening?" Ainsley whispers the question to Priscilla, confused at the sudden enmity from both sides.

"Oh, something about a bakery right across Orion's shop. He's been bickering about a parking spot and the daily fight with one of the bakery's employees. What a small world!" She laughs, trying to get a better look at the face that has driven Orion mad for the couple past weeks.

"Is that so?" Amanda Nowak, in a fight? To be fair, Ainsley does not know Amanda as she does the rest of her family. But as she sees the young woman, red on the face for a spot of pavement — there is amusement in the turning wheels of fate.

"Is that the twink next door you mentioned, Manda?" Hanna says, perhaps a bit too loudly as she adjusts her glasses to take a better look at Orion.

"The twink!?" Even Orion's laid-back facade breaks to make way for astronomical levels of pissed off. She has no right, even if it might be true.

"Twink!" Tommy emerges from the foliage to repeat the funny word, and Estelle loses it too.

"Ach, I don't need to take this. Nice meeting you, Ainsley, but I'm off." He throws his hands up as he leaves. "Jokes on you, Mandy, the parking spot is mine today!"

He shakes his keys in the air as he passes the door. Amanda makes a fist at him as she considers a backstabbing spell, but she backtracks. He wins, for now.

The people that remain, sans Amanda, burst into bubbly laughter before dispersing again to take on another day of hard work. Time for the finishing touches.

With the flower arrangements more than sorted, Priscilla gets started on the finishing touches for the festival. The planned white shimmery fabric cascading here and there almost feels like too much in her hands, but as she drapes it with care, it provides the perfect rest in between the explosion of colours from the flowers.

With Ainsley's help, they take the seats and tables that Ainsley had been kindly gifted and one by one, they place them across the patio, with enough to spare for the front garden as well for a break from the crowd.

The last task is to tie the ribbons to the birch tree at the heart of this festival. Priscilla had found the prettiest colour-changing satin in her latest trip to the craft store for a different project, and she had happily mixed it into the pack Ainsley had stored from past festivals.

Ainsley brings a ladder from a shed hidden in the back garden — so hidden that Priscilla had not even realised there was a shed. It's rustic but so solid Priscilla has no problem climbing it with a single hand to start tying the ribbons to the low-hanging branches.

"Hm. This would go faster if one of us could just fly." Edmund notes as the family makes to leave, their work in the kitchen being done for now.

"Don't even think about it, darling. Do you know how hard it was to glamour this place?" Estelle warns him as she walks them out. If he breaks the illusion and starts levitating, the spell ends right there and now. Hours of work down the drain, and the complete panic that would ensue for Priscilla.

"Listen to Estelle, Edmund." His mother chimes in. "Besides, I haven't seen Ainsley this excited about anything in a long time. Especially for May Day, of all things. Let her enjoy it at her own pace."

Estelle, Tommy and the Nowaks say their goodbyes amidst hugs and waves, leaving Ainsley and Priscilla to finish their work for the day.

The ribbons don't take that much longer, despite Edmund's quiet cry for optimal productivity. As they sit by one of the tables to take their work in, the sun finally dawns, despite the late hours of the night.

"It is quite impressive, isn't it? In just a fortnight's time these halls will be brimming with music and life. You should be proud, Priscilla. That is a night they won't soon forget."

They sit side by side, leaning onto each other as they look up at the beams of fading light coming through the leaves and branches.

"Hm. I can't help but feel like something is missing…" As they are, with the last rays of the day, the place looks incredible. But it won't last for as long as they need it, as they expect the party to extend until the small hours of the night for those who can stay.

They could turn all of the lights on the halls surrounding the patio, yes. But it wouldn't look quite right…

Priscilla stands and paces in thought. Could she bring some lights to drape with the flags up high? It's one solution, but she's still not sure it would quite fit.

She spots it, then. Amongst the flowers in between the ground and upper floor, almost hidden in their shadows. She takes the ladder from the tree and carefully repositions it for a better look — Ainsley in tow to provide her with more support on the ladder.

"What is that?" Priscilla asks, pushing flowers around with care to unearth it.

"Ah, you have found the oil lamps. They haven't exactly been used in quite a long time." Ever since the mansion had been fitted for electrical energy, however ago that was. They were abandoned then, only serving as wall decor.

"That's it! They're perfect, Ainsley. How do we light them up?" The light from those lamps will provide the perfect mood for the night. Oh, how were they just hiding in plain sight, blending in with the walls?

Priscilla notices something by the corner of her vision, though, so close to the arrangements now. She can see the rope Ainsley had helped her put up, the stems of the flowers curling around it,

But… Those weren't placed there by hand, knotted around it… Some of these flowers have sprouted directly from the wall she's leaning against right now, through the cracks in between the stone that makes it.

'… How?' is all she can think, but Ainsley interrupts her investigation.

"Follow me."

⌒ ୬ৎ ⌒

Ainsley takes Priscilla to the upper floor where they pass rows upon rows of empty bedrooms until they find the one Ainsley is looking for.

The wallpaper has long since faded, but Priscilla can make the faint silhouette of birds painted onto them along the height of her knees. It's one of the smallest rooms, and most of the furniture is covered in fabric to keep the significant layer of dust away.

Against a wall, chests, boxes and crates are stacked amidst backwards facing canvases. Are they paintings? Pictures? Portraits? Their frames have eroded over time, the golden cover peeling and mixing with the dust that lifts with their steps.

Ainsley's posture is different as she steps around the crates too, Priscilla notes. She's almost… Hesitant to be here.

"I can wait outside." Priscilla offers, holding Ainsley's arm to stop.

"No… No. Two pairs of eyes are better than one. I do apologise for the mess, however. I… I don't come to this room that often any more." Ainsley offers her a smile, but it is weak and her eyes are still plagued by something Priscilla cannot place.

They start rummaging through the objects there, looking for the lamp lighter and oil flask inside every chest and crate within sight — but no luck.

Ainsley is almost calling off the search, when she finally sees it — the long metal contraption with the trigger at the handle, lying covered by oil paints and brushes and thinner — the oil flask almost empty, but with enough for a trial run tonight. They can always get more for the festival.

"There we are."

Ainsley is ready to present them to Priscilla, fishing them out of the chest and closing it behind her. But as she turns, she finds Priscilla preoccupied with something else.

In her search, under another layer of fabric, Priscilla had come across a bassinet.

It isn't any ordinary bassinet, however — made of solid wood, it has been extensively carved and polished into intricate arabesques and animal figures of all sorts. At the intersection of pieces, however, the original shape of the wood shows — as if it had sprouted in this concave shape and dilapidated like a piece of marble, it fuses seamlessly with itself.

Priscilla traces the intricate woodwork along the sides. The mattress and blanket are still intact, if not faded. A small fabric doll with button eyes lies comfortably inside. It's a perfect picture of a distant memory, locked in time.

"Ainsley… Is this a nursery?" She comes to the logical conclusion, but there is little logic in the pain she feels for Ainsley.

Ainsley does not respond immediately. She places the lamp lighter and fluid flask down on top of the chest and joins Priscilla by the bassinet.

She stays silent for a moment, mulling over how to present such a painful part of her past to Priscilla. One long past her, yes, but the memories are fresh enough to be kept close — Priscilla deserves to know.

"It *was* a nursery, yes." Her eyebrows tighten in vulnerability.

"What happened?" Priscilla's voice is quiet.

"A great disease." Ainsley puts it simply. "It took us all by surprise. Within a single season, I was the only one left behind to tell the story."

"They?"

Ainsley lets out a gentle laugh, choosing to remember them as they were in their best moments, not their deathbed. She picks up the small felt doll from the blanket, cradling it in her arms as she cradled her own once.

"Her name was Eloise and her woodworking skills were unmatched, despite how little time she had to commit to her craft in between work and housekeeping in her former household. When her fiance left suddenly through the night, without notice or explanation, she was already carrying our dear Eli. She was turned down everywhere she looked for support, or even a listening ear — until she found me."

"It was rock bottom for her, I'm sure — as you well know my reputation from what your friend has told you." She manages a chuckle to escape her pained voice. "But very slowly, she learned to trust my friends, my family — and eventually, me."

"By Eli's birth, we were already madly in love. I provided the birch wood of this bassinet myself, but she shaped it into what it is now. It was a promise… That we would keep him safe and care for him, always. And so we did."

Ainsley grips the finely carved edge of the bassinet, trying to ground herself, but it's a distant pain, a scar left in its place forever — one of many. Priscilla places a single hand over hers, not daring to speak a single word, but not being strong enough to hold back her tears.

"After they passed, I couldn't bring myself to part with their things. I grieved, for too long perhaps, but I never forgot them."

She hasn't forgotten any of her other companions in her long, immortal life — all of them imparting a mark onto her heart as one by one they leave her behind. But she carries their memories, and the grief that comes with it proudly — a testament to life itself.

"I'm so sorry, Ainsley." Priscilla cannot begin to imagine how a tragedy like that would impact someone. That Ainsley, her sweet, kind Ainsley would have suffered so much…

"Do not be, Priscilla." Ainsley shakes her head, and they embrace, finding comfort in each other's arms. "I have made my peace with their deaths. I do not tell you such a story to burden you with the same pain I have had to battle — I do it so you are aware of where I come from, so we can grow from it."

With hearts still sore, they take the oil and lighter and lamp by lamp, no matter how unreachable it looks — they light them up.

One by one, the patio is lit in the soft yellow flicker. Tomorrow morning, the oil will have run out, and the flames will have extinguished.

No matter — they will be here to light them up again.

# Chapter 7

"Alright, that was the last invite, darling, and it's not even past noon." Estelle congratulates their group effort.

Their entire morning today was spent going from address to address in the city, handing out invites for May Day to all the guests that would be attending. They had all already been unofficially invited weeks ago, by phone call, text message or even word of mouth. The physical invites, neatly sealed with wax and the customary birch crest were just a formality at this point — and a good opportunity to greet friends old and new who Ainsley had not yet had the chance to see again.

They had already visited at least a dozen different shops selling a dozen different things by a dozen different families of all sorts, not to mention taken tea at a residence or two before they found themselves too full to accept any more. It had been wonderful to be welcomed so warmly by so many of her old friends, but even good hospitality can be too much.

"I am afraid you are mistaken, Estelle, my friend. There is still one last letter I must deliver."

Ainsley produces the same uniform sage green envelope they have been distributing so far. In its back, handwritten by Ainsley herself, is Priscilla's name.

"Oh, Ainsley my darling Ainsley, things are getting this serious between you two?" Estelle takes the invitation from her hand to inspect it and waves it around in an excited flourish before handing it back.

"I would like to think so, yes. At least, serious enough to the point where I cannot keep concealing my real nature from her, Estelle."

"You're taking down the glamour spells."

"I am taking down the glamour spells, yes." They say in unison.

"She has asked me for a date, today, at her favourite coffee shop. We'll head out to her home afterwards so we can watch today's episode of Emmerdale together, and I will tell her everything then." Ainsley states her plan.

"Emmerdale, huh? Dear, you two were really just made for each other." Estelle opens the door to her car, sitting on the driver's side and expecting Ainsley to follow suit.

When she doesn't find Ainsley with her but instead rummaging through her bag in search of something, she's puzzled. When Ainsley takes out a cheque book — of all things — from it, she's hysterical.

"What the hell are you doing, darling? Get in the car, I'll drive you up the road." She dares ask before imparting any judgement.

"The ride is appreciated, Estelle, but I must decline it. The fact that I only have one pair of shoes, and they're borrowed from you, has made me realise I'm in desperate need of some new pieces for my wardrobe. Especially if I want to impress Priscilla for our first date in the city."

"And you're gonna go shopping for them expecting to pay…"

"With a cheque, yes. Or would it be better to use cash? Do they still accept pounds or has the currency changed?" Ainsley asks, her years showing again.

Estelle can only shake her head, pursing her lips.

"Hm. Hm hm, get in the car, dear. You are not entering a single department store before we get you a proper contactless card." Even with Ainsley's taste in comfortability, she could not expect her to make good clothing choices after seventeen years away. She is in dire need of help, especially if she's going for something nice.

A *cheque!*

This is the day.

Ainsley has shown Priscilla so much of her world already — the forest, her home, her trust as she redecorated it for the festival, as she poured her heart open with her past.

What has Priscilla given back?

Today, this changes. Today, Priscilla is picking her up for a wonderful time in the city — a nice cup of coffee and then some cuddling on her sofa back at her flat.

She gets to dress up this time, choosing a nice and flowy summer dress in a delicate floral pattern. Her hair is accented by a simple pearl chain around a bun, matching her necklace and earrings perfectly. Even as she waits, she reapplies the soft peach lipstick against her car's rear mirror to keep her heart from overtaking her nerves.

Not that it makes a difference — As soon as she spots Ainsley emerging from the dirt path Priscilla herself had walked so many times now, it is as if nature parts itself in half to make way for its rightful Queen.

Her long sepia dress trails behind her in the grass, a simple cut gathered together at the higher waist in a ribbon. Her hair has been partially braided away from her face, giving deserved attention to her lovely freckled complex and the golden accessories that had become a staple in her recent ensembles.

She's royalty, straight from a fairytale book, here to grace Priscilla's mere mortal existence. She always has been.

'You look lovely today, Ainsley' or even a simple 'You humble me with your most holy presence, Your Majesty' would have been fine reactions. But all that Priscilla musters is —

"Woah…"

It works, because of course it does, and Ainsley almost blushes.

"I hope this is not too much. I've recently had a wardrobe refresh, and I may have gotten carried away.

"What? No, no, please, Ainsley. You're — This is perfect." Priscilla shakes herself out of her awe-induced stupor to form a proper sentence.

"I shall be honest, it has been a long time since I have been on a proper date — and even then, I am usually the one taking the other out, not the opposite. It's…"

"Weird?"

Ainsley chuckles.

"Different. Unexpected, perhaps, but a welcome sort of change." She has been the one in charge of so many other's lives, making the decisions and taking the wheels. It's refreshing to take a step back and let someone else make the choices.

It couldn't be more different for Priscilla — all her life, she has been the one ordered around, a thousand expectations placed on her shoulder. Taking Ainsley on this date, however small it seems, makes a world of difference to her.

"I promise you are in good hands, Ainsley. Just enjoy the day, yeah?"

Ainsley nods, and Priscilla opens the car door for her with an exaggerated curtsey, to Ainsley's amusement and delight.

This is going to be the best date of her life.

⌒ ↄ)ʕↄ ⌒

Her favourite café in town is a quaint little shop if you're only looking at its entrance — A simple glass door and a small display, with some seats scattered on the sidewalk.

But to the regulars, much like Priscilla is, well… They know there is more than meets the eye.

If you take the stairs by the till, after a short climb up you will find yourself by the building's terrace. The seats there are much more comfortable, especially under the relentless sun of this coming summer as you can find reprieve in the shade of a parasol. Up so high, the breeze is constant and the noise of the streets is just a distant buzz.

"What a breathtaking vista, Priscilla," Ainsley notes, almost enjoying being at the heart of the city when she can see it all from the safety of above. "It makes all of this noise almost… Tolerable."

"Really? I wouldn't know, I guess. I've lived all my life in big cities — when you're born in it, all the chaos just becomes background static."

"Have you never thought of moving closer to the country?" Ainsley asks, absent-mindedly, but looks directly at Priscilla.

"Careful there, Ainsley. If I didn't know any better, I'd assume you were asking me to move in." Priscilla jokes, but Ainsley knows that if it wasn't for proper society's rules, she might have considered offering by now.

Their food gets there by a contraption Ainsley hasn't seen in working condition for a good while — a service elevator, complete with a gentle 'ding!' as their food arrives.

Between the assortments of muffins, bagels, cakes and biscuits — and their respective drinks — they have enough to last through a nice, long conversation.

And it will be a long one, Priscilla is sure.

"I can see why this place is so special to you. If I lived so close to such good food and ambience, I too would keep it close to my heart."

Priscilla smiles but dismisses that statement with a head shake.

"It is one of the nicer places in this town, and so close to my flat too, but that's not the main reason why I love it so much." She explains. "This is the first place I visited after fleeing my past home — if I can even call it that — when I finally felt like… Well, like myself."

Ainsley places her drink down, realising where this conversation is going.

"You don't need to tell me anything you are not comfortable reliving in memory, Priscilla. You will not lose me if you choose to keep this." Ainsley reassures her, holding her hand over the table. But she places her cup down, looking at the steam rising from it as she tilts her head.

"But I do! I do... After you laid your heart out to me and let me into such an intimate part of your past... I saw my own struggle in you, despite our stories being so different. We're just like May Day flowers as well, when you think about it, you know? Pretty when in bloom, all colourful in the spring, but no one sees the winter we had to go through to get there — because we don't let them. We're there to dazzle, not to deprive."

Ainsley knows this well — when you are such an important figure, when so many look to you for guidance, it is so easy to lose yourself in the projected image you have created.

Priscilla looks up to the sunny sky as an airplane cuts the clouds up above.

"They should be nearing their sixties now, I think. My parents, that is, not that I would know how they're doing now. I broke that bridge the day I moved here — blocked their numbers everywhere. I haven't heard a peep since, but they somehow got a hold of my address and they still send me gifts from time to time, to try and win me back. Mom, especially."

"Your parents? What have they done to compel you to flee across the ocean, Priscilla?" She does not ask to question — but to be horrified. Ainsley has seen her fair share of abusive homes, and they never cease to make her blood boil.

"Oh, it wasn't just one thing. Years and years of parading me like a doll, of placing expectation upon expectation on my shoulders — of bragging about how many extracurricular activities I had signed up for while scolding me for not being top of my class when the guests were gone. By the time I was eight, they had already planned my entire life for me.

So, the daydreaming started. That place stopped being my home as soon as I imagined a new one up — with unicorns and gnomes and kingdoms to save. Somewhere I actually had a say on things."

Priscilla laughs, but it's a hollow one, Ainsley notices. She looks to the horizon, lost in that dreadful place again.

"My teenage years were spent mostly in depression when I wasn't inside my head. I tried to run away a few times then, but they would always send the police after me. I would pay by having all of my clothes and makeup thrown in the bin. It's how I got so good at handcrafts… Fixing mouse bites and tears and stains is a sure way to develop skills, fast." She tries the joke, an absentminded half smile with it, but Ainsley doesn't laugh with her.

"The last two years with them were the worst — I got a job at a hardware store, and I saved every single penny that got there while they signed my name for all the medical universities in our area. I refused each and every acceptance letter, and the punishment became… Well, physical." She dares not elaborate. "Orion was there for me through all of that too, helping me plan the night of my escape and getting everything ready on his side.

That was eight years ago, give or take. When he took me to this exact coffee shop as soon as I had landed, I was exhausted and jet-lagged, and all I had with me was a suitcase with my documents and some keepsakes. I looked around at this small city, just over there —" She points to a corner with potted plants overlooking the main square. "And then it clicked — I was… I was *free*."

Free, truly, for the first time ever.

Free to eat ice cream. Free to wake up late on a Sunday. Free to make a mistake, and apologise for it without fearing for her life. Free to exist in the same room as another person and expect nothing of it — just the silence, a comfortable one for the first time.

Free!

Free to go window shopping on a nice afternoon, just like she takes Ainsley now after they finish their tea. Free to stroll around the city, with no particular direction in mind and without the paranoia of being spotted and tattled on, to be left with no dinner that night. Free to take the woman (or not quite so) she loves —

The one she *loves*! Ah… She loves her.

To take her hand in her own, without guilt or shame. To sit with her by a bench on the river's islands, under the tall shadows of a mighty oak and look at the river make its languid course. To kiss her, again and again, and for it to never be enough. For her to kiss her back, just as often.

*Free.*

"So… I may just look like a pretty flower, but I still have plenty of thorns to show. And now you know about them."

Ainsley hums in thought, but the perfect answer has already been uttered before.

"It is not about being perfect, for yourself or anyone else, for that matter." She quotes. "What matters is the journey, together, for as long as we will have each other."

"Hey —" Priscilla recognises it instantly, looking up from her comfortable lean against Ainsley's shoulder, and they laugh.

"I am paraphrasing, of course. But on that day you showed me such an immeasurable amount of compassion, Priscilla, without the faintest idea of what ailed me so, yet you did." Ainsley rests her head on Priscilla's. "All I ask you is to extend the same forgiveness to yourself."

She tries. She really does — that is all she has been doing since that day eight years ago.

Today, she succeeds a little better.

⌒ ʒℓ ◌

It's about six on the clock by the time they decide to make their way to Priscilla's flat.

Ainsley ducks through the threshold, being unaccustomed to such short wall heights as Priscilla welcomes her into her small piece of heaven — a one-bedroom, one-bath on the upper floor of her complex.

It's quaint and comfortable, in the way Priscilla does best — decorated to the brim, every nook and cranny exuding the same care she has put everywhere else in her life. The soft pastels and creams are tinted by the filtered sunlight coming in through the curtains and her scent permeates every room.

To think she put this place together, from scratch, in just a few years… Her skills, her resilience truly knows no bounds.

"So… What do you think? Not as fancy as a mansion, I know, but even a renting tenant can have some fun."

Priscilla takes Ainsley from room to room, leaving the tiny balcony in the living room last so she can open the sliding doors for some ventilation. The curtains wave and billow with the wind that makes its way through the flat, and thankfully the sun doesn't hit them directly — leaving way for a nice view of the river bridge over the treeline of her shared backyard.

Ainsley embraces her from behind, resting her chin on Priscilla's head and taking in the view.

"It's very you." She states, plainly.

In any other context, it might even have been rude. But this is Priscilla, the one and only. Ainsley knows that, and so does she.

She had been so strong until now, too — exposing all the sore spots of her soul with grace and poise, without shedding a tear either. But now, under Ainsley's tight embrace and such a raw compliment, she breaks.

Ainsley says nothing, simply tightening her hold as Priscilla's knees buckle under her building sobs. She holds her, for however long she needs, kissing her temple and whispering comforts into her ear. Just as Priscilla had felt her pain for Ainsley's lost family, now Ainsley does it too for the one Priscilla was never afforded in the first place.

In Ainsley's arms, Priscilla finds a calm she has never felt before. She lets everything that has been building up in her soul out, knowing she has people who care for her, now more than ever — Orion, his family, and now Ainsley.

She will be OK. They all will.

Ainsley reconsiders inviting Priscilla to the ball.

She is much calmer now, with her tears mostly dried by Ainsley's own handkerchief. But she is clearly in no state to receive any world-breaking news from someone she had come to trust so much.

Ainsley chastises herself for taking so long to tell Priscilla about magical folk like herself. It may be the general consensus, to wait until it develops into something serious, for everyone's safety… But there is nothing average about their relationship, is there?

Now, she fears for the worst — for absolutely breaking Priscilla's heart as she finds something so unexpected about Ainsley, yet so integral to who she is.

So integral to why their time together might have a due date.

How would she react? Would she run in fear, like so many have done? Or would she —

Ainsley winces.

Priscilla had explained about her sudden, but very serious case of what she called, scientifically, 'maladaptive daydreaming'. How she had only recently put a name to it in therapy, despite struggling with hours and hours of her time lost in dissociation — or perhaps in refuge — in the made-up scenarios in her head since she was eleven.

How many of those dreams involved creatures of lore much like Ainsley, and Estelle, and Zack, and the many other folks living in this city, right under her nose, all this time? Will this set her back, and cause another episode?

Or, more optimistically — would she embrace it, fully? Would she take Ainsley as she is, vines and branches exposed? Her knight in shining armour — or more specifically, though bark — ready to swoop her from her feet and protect her too?

Ainsley knows not. So, for now, the green envelope stays in her bag as she holds Priscilla tight. At this moment, that is more than enough.

"I have a funny confession to make, actually."

Priscilla says very quietly, looking to the horizon, and tiny hiccups interrupt her tiny chuckles.

"The first time I saw you, on that first day I went to your place — I think… I thought I saw something."

Ainsley freezes, but Priscilla's eyes remain looking forward, and she sees it again — that sparkle. She knows it now, so well, and she's certain that while Priscilla's conscience is here, her mind is long gone somewhere else.

"What did you see?" She asks, but Ainsley knows what Priscilla is talking about.

"You know what? Nothing important, just my mind playing tricks on me, another episode. It just shows how annoying they've been. Don't worry about it." Priscilla brushes it off, thinking it might not be appropriate to bring it up now — she too doesn't want to ruin a perfect moment between them.

But Ainsley breaks their comfortable cuddle to face her, to look deep into her eyes.

"You saw me." It's almost a whisper, something she's not too sure of herself.

"What?" Priscilla smiles, but her brows furrow in confusion.

It couldn't have been. It's not possible.

"What did you see, Priscilla?" Again, so quiet, but loud enough to be read. Pleading.

She needs to think for a moment. How will she even put that vision into words? Especially in a way that won't lead Ainsley to think she's absolutely off the rails.

Can she trust — Of course she can.

She has.

"That day, the first thing I saw when I came in was the tree. That beautiful birch that you have in your place, the one we tied all those ribbons to... It took my breath away, I had never seen something like it before. As I walked closer, well... It's like one of its branches came into view, and then it *moved*."

Priscilla lifts her own hand, mimicking the movement she saw then. Her arm against the bright blue sky is much shorter and plumper. Ainsley's own joins into the dance, extending past the balcony and meeting Priscilla's.

How uncannily similar Ainsley's movements are there, as her freckled hand intertwines with hers... But more importantly, how perfectly they fit together.

"That was already unusual, but then I saw more. More branches, more vines, a face. Lips, as dark as the striped bark — and those eyes..."

Priscilla looks at Ainsley again, their gazes colliding.

"They looked just like yours — but they were inky black, like a galaxy. A universe you can wander in..."

They both feel it then, the static surrounding their bodies, the way the wind encases them in complete silence.

She knows.

Ainsley moves her free hand to her earring, the pendant once humming with magic — now it stills. Like the oasis mirage on a scalding day, it fades and disintegrates with the sun's rays, leaving only the truth behind.

Her auburn hair unfolds into vines of the same length, now much more verdant as the summer approaches fast; her freckles dissolve to make space for long dark stripes that frame her face, tints her lips and concentrate on her hands; her eyes once a light amber widen to accommodate the vastness of existence.

On her hand, the remnants of her earring lay shattered.

"You saw me, Priscilla."

Priscilla takes a step back, mouth agape, but her knees don't tremble and she doesn't wince. She looks at her, the real her, from head to toe, taking in every single detail that she can, committing it to memory forever.

She brings a hand to Ainsley's face, and although it looks so different, it still feels soft if not bumpier as it shifts from complete white to a dark grey. She still smells of wild fruit and lemongrass and she still looks at Priscilla with such adoration, if not more now.

"Ainsley…"

It really is her, Ainsley, her Ainsley — the same Ainsley that listened to her, that took her to places she could never have imagined. The same Ainsley that held her as she cried just an hour ago.

Ainsley.

"Tell me the truth. Everything. Please."

Yet she says nothing else, and the uncharacteristic silence troubles Ainsley.

She does not regret telling Priscilla — come what may, it is the right choice. But now the truth is out of her hands, and there's nothing else she can do but wait.

Ainsley takes the green envelope she had been keeping so close and places it on the table.

"I understand if you would like to cut ties. But you helped bring this festival to life, and I would love nothing more than to at least see you there so you can see the fruit of your work. Feel free to extend the invite to Orion and the rest of your family."

Ainsley makes to leave then, standing up and heading for the door, a knot stuck in her throat that she pushes down. But something about what she says breaks Priscilla out of her stupor.

"Cut ties!? Ainsley, what are you saying?" Priscilla rises from her chair suddenly and Ainsley turns back.

"I have lied to you, Priscilla — whatever my reasons, I would completely understand if you were to take offence and wish to distance yourself." Ainsley explains, adjusting her posture.

"Well, I don't. Why would I? You were just trying to look out for yourself." Priscilla, more than anyone, would understand keeping her mouth shut for self-preservation. "It's just… Well…"

She walks to the sofa just behind Ainsley and grabs the crocheted throw that was spread over the arms of the furniture.

"It's a lot. I just need some time to organise my thoughts." Priscilla wraps Ainsley with the throw so she has something to conceal herself now that the spell has been broken, and smiles. "But it doesn't mean I am leaving you."

Ainsley sighs in relief and smiles too.

"Take all the time you need." For Priscilla, she would wait another lifetime.

# Chapter 8

God, Priscilla is exhausted when she gets home. She wishes she had had any time to process all of the revelations she came to yesterday, she really does — but the life of a self-employed worker stops for no one. If she doesn't get her butt off of bed in the morning, her work gets delayed, and if her work gets delayed, she misses her deadlines and she doesn't get paid.

It's a frustrating reality, and one she would change in a heartbeat — but here we are. Better make the most of it and try not to sink into despair.

After she drove Ainsley back and was left with just herself, alone in her flat, she almost regretted asking for time. She still had so many questions left and no one there to answer any of them.

To be honest, Priscilla was actually OK with the revelation. Too OK, which was just freaking her out.

Her relationship with Ainsley, when she thought she was just another human being like any other, was already something you don't really get often. Priscilla already felt so incredibly lucky to have met her, and it already felt like a dream come true.

But now? This is something straight out of fairy tale books. A dryad, an immortal of many names and many faces and many lives who happens to have taken an interest in her—

Simple, mortal, perfectly human Priscilla.

No, she won't downplay her own strengths—she knows she's an attractive woman with a killer sense of fashion, valuable skills and a sweet personality to top it all off.

So why is she still so shaken?

She loves Ainsley, and that has not changed. She still finds her attractive — if not even more, now. She's perfect, so perfect.

Reality can't be this good, can it?

How can Priscilla be sure this isn't just another daydream?

She sighs, opening the door to her bathroom to find the twists she had gotten a couple of days ago finally dry from their wash. She sends a voice message to Orion as she turns her shower on to warm it up for her wash day.

"My twists are ready, and I remember someone promised to help me with them."

His response is almost instant.

"Shit, that was fast. Dinner at yours, date details for dessert? I have a lot to tell you about that arse Amanda — "

"Yo, is that Pri? How's it going with what's-her-name? Orion won't tell me anything about it, he just keeps whining about some girl he's been fighting at recess, it's so booooring!"

"Shut your hole, Cass! It's none of your business!"

Thuds, clothes rustling. Priscilla laughs as she carefully transfers her hair to her coffee table, her eyes unconsciously darting to that green envelope Ainsley had left her, still there.

She had read it more times than she could count the past night, but it contained nothing she already didn't know — much less any answers. On the back, it says:

'To Priscilla and family.'

She needs to tell them.

"Date details for dessert, absolutely. You're invited too, Cass. Gosh, I have so much to share. Don't leave me waiting."

She puts her phone down and gets started. A nice dinner and a second (and third) opinion while she gets a makeover will put everything in perspective.

"Aye, I know," Cass says nonchalantly.

"You know!?" Priscilla and Orion exclaim in unison.

By the time her siblings had gotten there, Priscilla had already washed and done most of the parting on her hair. Now she sits with Orion by the sofa — she had gotten comfortable on the floor so he could reach the back while she took care of the front, and they could both watch a show on the TV.

Cass, Orion's older sister and certified badass, tinkers away in the kitchen as she whips a mystery curry for dinner.

For the past half hour, Priscilla had done her best to relay all the vital parts of what happened yesterday. She skipped over a lot of the details about her past, as both Orion and Cass are already familiar with most of it.

But as she begins describing the reveal, describing the real appearance of Ainsley, the tone shifts. Orion thinks she's just fucking around with them, telling a story just to be funny. Priscilla expected that, of course.

What she doesn't expect is his older sister to turn her back to the stove she had been tending, and say exactly just that:

"Aye, I know."

The room goes quiet except for the low blabbering of the television. Priscilla and Orion turn in tandem, both incredulous but for completely different reasons.

"Fuck off, Cass, that's not funny." Orion turns back to Priscilla. "What are you even on about, Pri? That just sounds like more of your daydreaming."

"You know?" Priscilla ignores Orion.

"Aye. I dated this guy for a while — didn't work out in the end, but we had the same conversation. I'll say, I took it much worse than you are, love." She points a sauce-covered wooden spoon at Priscilla from over the island counters dividing the kitchen and living room. "So your Ainsley is an immortal dryad, huh? Must be nice. I hear she's a big deal around town too."

"You have to be kidding me. Who? Where are the cameras? This isn't funny." Orion isn't laughing while he looks for hidden lenses around the room, but Priscilla and Cass aren't laughing either.

"She is… I honestly didn't know what to think at first, but it's good to know I'm not imagining something that isn't there. Thanks, Cass." Priscilla smiles, and Cass gives her a wink back.

Her heart calms, the conversation giving her a bit of peace in the middle of the storm as her body relaxes against the sofa. Her head rests back on Orion's legs as they look at each other.

"You're serious." It finally dawns for upside-down Orion. "No joke?"

"I'm serious, Orion," Priscilla confirms. "You know I wouldn't joke around about this."

He looks around in thought.

"And you're sure she's not actually the ghost of the cairns?

Priscilla laughs.

"You're dating a dryad? Ainsley. The dryad. The dryad Ainsley. A birch spirit, inside a birch tree."

"I am!" Priscilla brings her hands to her cheeks in disbelief, smiling from ear to ear. "Oh gosh, I need to talk to her. We didn't really leave that date on a cheery note."

"Forget that, you can do it tomorrow — I have an urgent question." Orion puts his hands over Priscilla's on her face to keep her from wandering off before answering him.

"What?"

"She has vines."

"…Yes." They're the nicest, most vibrant shade of green too… Oh, do they change with the seasons as well? Did she miss all her flowers blooming under that spell, the

leaves appearing on them as she woke up from winter?…
What a shame.

"Can she move them?"

Can she? Just another question to ask her tomorrow…

"I don't know. Why?"

But Orion widens his eyes, waiting for her to pick
some sort of cue up.

"…What?"

He sighs in frustration, shutting his eyes.

"Get there faster."

It still takes her a moment more, and she pouts — but
when she does get it, she leaps up from her seat, a hand
over her mouth to cover her shock.

"No — You don't think —"

She's scandalised, but can't take her mind off the
possibility. God knows she has seen weirder stuff online,
but if this is true —

Oh my. Vines.

Her gasp is audible. Orion falls back on the couch,
heave-laughing until he runs out of air.

"Oh absolutely nothing is off the table here, let me
tell you." Cass laughs as well but it's much more contained.
She speaks from experience too, holding her fingers up for
dramatics. "My guy? He had two."

"Two!?" Priscilla exclaims.

"Two!?" Orion sits up, mumbling in indignation.
"Bloody greedy bastard!"

It's too much, all over again, but in a simply exciting
way now. She sits back on the couch, mindlessly applying
more styling gel to her hair.

"You two were supposed to help, not put more thoughts into my head!" She huffs. Ainsley had already turned Priscilla into an incoherent puddle with her perfectly regular human-like appendages. What kind of damage could she do with —

She doesn't dare give that line the time. She can't. She'll combust.

"You're really telling me you had a complete existential crisis with the cons there but you never thought about any of the pros? Ach, Pri, never change." Orion laughs, and they resume their work with the twists in between chuckles.

Oh, but she will. In fact, she can already feel it happening.

Vines…

⁂

Ainsley tries to keep her mind off Priscilla. She does.

She occupies her day with her usual routine — Waking up in the wee hours of the day so she has enough time to prepare some breakfast — mushrooms, vegan sausages and a couple of pieces of toast this morning — which she decides to enjoy on her early hike through the woods.

Those daily hikes serve a twofold purpose — The main one being a sort of surveillance, although perhaps that would be too harsh a word. It would be more accurate to describe it as something akin to a shepherd looking after their flock, a watchful eye simply checking if nothing is amiss. The second is very simple, yet not less important —

She just thoroughly enjoys them.

It's a pleasure that has never faded, simply wandering the woods, letting her two feet reach places her branches never could but that her roots have known for long.

She still needs to take Priscilla on a proper scenery hike, too. There are so many places left to show her — but Ainsley does not let her mind wander back to Priscilla, not now.

She stops only to have her food by the old ruins of a castle fort, built sometime in the early fourteen hundreds on one of the islands of this loch. She tries to remember the folk posted there, then, to place any faces that she might have seen in her wanders at that time — to no avail. When you live this long, some memories are bound to slip, and the further away from the present, the less she is able to retain.

She dwells no longer than needed, however, and promptly resumes her wanders.

It takes her a good part of the morning to reach the seashore but the salty winds of deeper sea invigorate her spirits once more. She can feel the drag of the vast distance from her spirit tree, weighing her down and almost pulling her back, the dirt turning into sand making poor bedding for her roots to reach. She endures nonetheless, finding respite as she spots a familiar face: her old friend, William.

They talk about nothing and everything, catching up and making sure he will be attending May Day this weekend. He wouldn't miss it, but he says he half expected Ainsley's estate to be gone by now. Hilltop has been nothing but ruthless in their pursuit of William's lovely house by the cliff overlooking the firth.

'I cannae do it — where would ma lassie and I go?' He says, looking to his only and one companion, Marjorie

— an old but beautiful thing, his fishing boat for the good portion of a few decades.

They share their anxieties about this situation, promising to help each other if Hilltop decides they are desperate enough for illegal means of acquisition. Ainsley does not like to expect the worst, but time has trained her well to be prepared for it, at least.

Her way back home seems to be uneventful, if not a bit harder than usual — the sun peaks in the sky and not even the thickest parts of the forest are free from its toll. The wind offers little comfort, just as warm as the ground that cracks with dry branches and leaves as Ainsley treads over them.

As she wanders around those woods she knows like the back of her hand, she starts noticing the small details. Things that, perhaps, would slip any other's perception, but that she can spot instantly.

How the families of swans that call her forest's lake home would fill it every summer, after migrating back from their winter down south — but that now are few and far in-between, only a couple of groups scattered across the forest.

How every couple of miles or so, Ainsley will run into an open meadow. She expects it to be brimming with flora and fauna alike, for the flowers to be blooming fully and for the bumblebees to be buzzing around, busy working their nectar collection — only to be welcomed by a patch of shrubbery so dry, so beaten and lifeless and brown her heart skips a beat.

She attempts to revive them, drawing from her magic to bring colour to it once more, to make it bloom — yet she knows it's a fool's errand.

For she is only one, and despite her efforts, neither the bees nor the missing swans might ever show up again.

She diverts her path and reevaluates her plans for the evening to investigate it further, climbing her way to where she knows the starting point of a local burn should be. This font of water trickles down the cairn directly into the river, and in extreme summers like this, it can be the difference between a simple low tide to a complete drought. The forest depends on this river for its water supply and every person in the city does too — she knows the state of this creek will be decisive in telling her how much of a crisis this following year will be in.

As she arrives at that peak, her heart sinks. She looks for it everywhere, double-checking she isn't misremembering the area, or that it didn't change its location to somewhere nearby in the decades she has been away. But it is no use —

All she finds is the dry dirt, the dead leaves, and the overbearing sun on her back.

The water is completely gone.

A knot forms inside her chest. And, as she aimlessly walks back home, she finally starts placing the discomfort she has been feeling, the years on end she has lost to time, into a theory.

*The 15th of October, 1954.*
*Ainsley, my friend, how happy I am to hear from you.*
*As I write this letter, war brews all around my wetlands. Yet my people and I hold our ground firmly, hand in hand around Mai Hing Sam, knowing it will pass as all other wars have.*

*We are all very sorry to hear of your predicament, but I'm afraid my sleep has not felt any different this year. As soon as the floods of July start, as always.*

*But I can feel it in the air, Ainsley. The wind currents are changing. The water seems to rise higher and higher. Something is happening, but I don't know what either.*

*I hope it passes soon too.*

*Your friend,*
*Phoukhong*

*03/09/1960*

*Ainsley! Thank you for your kind wishes.*

*The earthquake has taken much from us, but we are strong, and we survived.*

*I feel your plight. Our Alerce told me to sleep as we rebuilt our houses. I did what I could, but I woke in August, and my family had already taken care of the rest. I can't imagine waking up a whole month later. Alone.*

*Tragedy is part of our life, Ainsley. Take it from me, we will live to see many more. Even if the winter is longer, or the summer worse. I see it too, here. We will stand tall, and see it through.*

*Have faith.*

*Your sister, always.*
*Liwen.*

*January the 31st, 1971*

*Oh, we've missed your letters, Ainsley! How are you?*

*Don't worry about us, Nusiiku and I have been through so much worse. As long as we have each other, we will be alright. We will protect our trees with our own lives!*

*But we do understand what you're writing us about. Some days, not even the shade of our baobabs can withstand the temperatures. Between you and I, I think I'm about to lose one of my core stems. My tree isn't giving as much fruit this year. But I can't possibly tell my love any of this, she's already knee-deep into her worldwide warming thesis she's writing, and I can't give her more reason to be so fatalist about our fate. We have to hope for a better tomorrow.*

*Our bark is tough and our spirits are durable, Ainsley! Never forget that! I believe you will someday be completely back to normal, with my entire soul.*

*Hugs and kisses.*
*Nangula.*

Ainsley cannot keep going.

She lets the silent tears fall from her face to the letter she currently holds, grieving all over again for the loss of her kin. Alone, hunched over an old wooden box in another empty room of her estate — she makes a mental note to check up on Nussiku, Phoukhong, Liwen, and the many other dryads scattered around this Earth. She hopes the world has treated them kindly in these past two decades she has been gone.

As she folds and organises her correspondence to store it again and put it away with care, she utters a small prayer for the well-being, before a melodic ring from the ground floor breaks her meditation.

Priscilla? It could be. In the name of creation, she hopes it is.

She wipes her tears, and with unclouded eyes, she takes their message to heart.

Normally, it would be no problem at all, being so far away from her landline. But with all the decorations laid out in her patio and the ribbons around her — it all makes it quite hard to call upon her tree's vines so she can fling herself to the ground floor. She dares not risk the possibility of ruining the perfect picture that had been conjured for the festival, so she rushes down the stairs with all the care in the world.

Perhaps it's due time for her to purchase one of those mobiles for herself.

She reaches her living room with a few rings left. She picks it up, and the rush is made worthwhile right there.

"Ainsley!"

"Priscilla…" Her Priscilla, with her voice full of life and energy again. Her joy is just the balm for her soul that Ainsley needed. "How glad I am to hear you once more. What can I do for you, my world?"

Priscilla laughs on the other side and how happy it makes Ainsley — it's unimaginable.

"You sound like you are in a good mood."

"I am, now that you have called." She chooses not to sour the moment, not now. "To what do I owe the pleasure?"

"I can't speak a lot right now, I'm heading into a meeting with some fancy-pants sorts, but… I was wondering if you were free tonight?" Ainsley can hear the quiet chatter and typing sounds of an office in the background. "I have so many questions — if you'll have me."

Oh, for Priscilla? She has all the time in the world.

"Of course — would you be willing to come up the road? I shall handle dinner preparations this time."

"That sounds incredible — gosh I didn't even have time for lunch today…"

"Then a feast it is. I hope this meeting does not drain you further."

"Oh, I've been through so much worse. Knowing I get to see you at the end of the day makes it better."

Ainsley tries to still the butterflies that start flying around in her stomach, to no avail.

"Oh god, here we go. I'll see you later, yeah?"

They both say their goodbyes quickly so Priscilla isn't late for her appointment, leaving Ainsley in the silence of her mansion once more.

But she isn't alone, is she? All around her, the birds sing, the forest sways, the television hums. In a moment, she will start her dinner preparations, and the sound of the chopping board and the clicking silverware will accompany her. And, in a couple of hours, Priscilla will be here.

Her laughter will fill these halls and brighten Ainsley's day once more.

This is her chance, Ainsley realises, to explain everything to Priscilla. To make her understand Ainsley. The transition can be difficult, but she will do her best to offer a comfortable place for Priscilla to get accustomed to it all — a nice atmosphere so she can feel safe to ask all her questions — so they can fully connect.

That is all she can do now.

# Chapter 9

What a day.

Priscilla misses the slow, laid-back pace of working on May Day preparations — today she has not stopped even to breathe properly. As she finally exits this briefing meeting for — surprise! — another beige-looking corporate party, her eyes suffer from the bright lights and she definitely has a slight headache because of them.

It matters not, she's out of there for now — work can wait until tomorrow.

As it is, her mind is already swarming with these questions. She has so much she wants to talk about with Ainsley… And, in truth, she simply misses her. So as she finally gets to her flat, she wastes no time — a shower, a spray of her favourite perfume, a light face of makeup, and one of her nicer sets of lingerie.

Her choice of clothing takes the longest, a nagging thought slowing her down and making her believe things that are not true. She holds a few options against her body, imagining the complete looks as she looks at herself in her bedroom's wall-length mirror.

It's no good.

Too prude, what are you trying to hide?

Too slutty, cover up more.

You'll look huge.

What are you even thinking? Put that down.

Give up. It's not worth it.

You're not worth it.

Priscilla catches herself before she spirals — she won't let herself go there.

She takes a deep breath and makes a choice — A snug dress in a muted rosé gold, and simple black pumps to withstand the short walk in the grass. To tie it all together, she pulls some of her twists back with a thin silken ribbon. Nothing too glamorous, but just dazzling enough for a dinner date.

But it could be more.

A beautiful Regency dress in yellow, peonies on her hat, and silky elbow-long opera gloves on her arms. Wings accent her back, long and feathery wings that she keeps close to herself for protection.

Suddenly, she is no longer in her room. Surrounded by woods — Ainsley's woods — she is no longer Priscilla, the event decorator.

She wanders, alone, in search of her castle.

'Lost, Princess?' A familiar voice echoes.

This, too, isn't Ainsley. But her long, white, speckled limbs embrace Priscilla from behind, encasing her chest and her waist tightly — her breath right at Priscilla's ear as it hitches.

'I'm right where I need to be.'

*Late.* Priscilla is so late.

"Shit."

She doesn't know how long that episode lasted exactly, but as she grabs her purse and keys and darts out of her door, the sun has already started to set.

She takes all her frustrations out with a knock on the steering wheel of her car, and she drives.

This is the last thing she needs right now, for her mind to blend and confuse reality with fantasy. The line has never been thinner for Priscilla, and she fears she might lose herself in it again.

The one saving grace is that she knows — it's *alright.* Just as Orion and the rest of his family had been patient with her with her episodes throughout the years, Ainsley, too, will understand. She cares for Priscilla, deeply, and if she shows up slightly late to their date it won't be the end of the world.

So, she breathes deeply and turns her head to the night ahead of her.

She makes just enough time to make a quick stop at that one bakery right across Orion's workshop, and she prays to all that is holy in this world that he doesn't spot her. Despite his personal vendetta with that girl Amanda, well — they just make incredible sweets at Nowak's Bakery. Orion had sent Priscilla in to buy some of their products so he could bad mouth them to hell — but all that managed to do was make him frustrated he couldn't find a single flaw, and hook her up for life.

In she goes, and out she comes with a small blackberry cheesecake for two — the perfect dessert for the dinner Ainsley would currently be preparing. That should do it.

She places it gently on the passenger seat of her car and drives out of the city.

On her way up the hill, she tries to make a list of all the questions she needs to be answered — but too soon they just turn into gibberish in her mind. All that is left is the prospect of a peaceful night with Ainsley — an Ainsley with bark for skin and green foliage on her head — but Ainsley nonetheless. Priscilla knows the questions are there, and they will come eventually. Ainsley will answer, and Priscilla will understand.

However much she has played and replayed that scene on her balcony, unfolding every layer she can find, sipping every detail she has retained — it just isn't enough. She needs to see Ainsley again, the real Ainsley, to feel what she has to feel in this new situation and come to a conclusion.

And she does. Ainsley is there, right at the front door, vines and all — dressed in a silken turtle-necked tunic, finely embroidered with arabesques in its entirety, along its edges — a white apron still wrapped around her front. Ainsley waits for her — or so Priscilla thinks, but only for a moment.

As she approaches, dessert in hand, she can see Ainsley's body language better.

She's… tense. Beside her, as she opens the wide front doors, she sees another figure. Neither Ainsley nor this mysterious guest realise Priscilla is there, and she can hear them discussing something — enmity seeping out of Ainsley's glare.

⁕

Dinner preparations are almost done — Ainsley had finished making the sides and the salad after putting the pie in the oven. If she has timed it right, the pie will be ready and cooled in time for Priscilla's arrival.

She takes this brief respite from the heat of her kitchen to go to her room and dress in something nicer. She has already set up the table in her dining space with a nice tablecloth, some of her finer china, and of course, a nice centrepiece with white candles just waiting to be lit.

But her makeover is suddenly and very rudely interrupted by a knock on her front door.

It cannot be Priscilla yet — it would be far too early. She is not expecting anyone else to visit, as even Estelle would have the decency to call ahead of time.

So who, then?

Ainsley waits for no answer as another knock bangs against the door. From her room's balcony overlooking the flowering patio, she summons a vine and elegantly slides down. On her ear, she preemptively wears another glamouring item — the other side of the one Priscilla had rendered useless.

Now completely human to most senses again, she opens her doors just enough to make out whoever requires her attention at such an inopportune time.

Ainsley does not recognize whoever this is. Hair slicked back on a millimetrically precise cut, sensible black frames and eyes that could scare any child into obedience — wearing a perfectly tailored suit, they stand by her front stairs, a suitcase in one hand and the other tucked away in their pocket.

"Ainsley Wood?" They ask.

"That will rather depend on who is currently asking."

The stranger produces a business card from their pocket. There is plenty of information on its back, but all Ainsley cares to absorb is a name —

"It is a pleasure to meet you. My name is Blair Ingram and I am here on behalf of Gray Granite."

Before tossing it somewhere she doesn't mind over her shoulder.

She has, of course, heard of Gray Granite — who hasn't? One of the biggest conglomerates currently running the world. Not even Ainsley, two decades removed from reality, has missed their presence on the news. They have strings attached to everything and everyone.

And now, they are trying to snag Ainsley as well.

"I was ready for Hilltop to send someone, not Gray Granite, so I must admit your presence here is surprising." She straightens her back, acknowledging the size of her opponent.

"I can see the confusion — Hilltop is merely a subsidiary of Gray Granite. They were scouting the region for us, with their local branch doing a fantastic job if I might add. Which brings us to this visit. May I enter?" She motions to the door.

But Ainsley does not budge from her spot.

"Normally, I would eagerly invite you in for a spot of tea and biscuits, but you see — I am entertaining tonight. So, unfortunately, I must decline." She musters her best fake smile. "Have a nice day, Mrs. Ingram. Ta ta."

Ainsley moves to close the door, but a perfectly polished shoe catches it before she can fully do so. A single eye is all that is visible of this woman through the small space left open, and she looks Ainsley dead in the eyes, that striking gaze almost piercing even Ainsley's impenetrable poise.

"I am aware of Ms. Cardoso's visit. I am also aware she is not anywhere near us yet."

"How do you —" Ainsley cannot believe what she is hearing. Have they been *spying* on her? On Priscilla? Her stomach turns at the thought, a sneer breaking her face.

"I am great at my job, Ms. Wood — but I am an even greater fortune teller," Blair explains as if reading Ainsley's thoughts, her neutral expression unchanging.

She might as well have.

Blair is a witch.

Ainsley lets out a dry laugh, and takes her earring off, revealing her real appearance to an unphased Blair.

"Look, I will be candid with you, Ms. Wood. I am currently jet-lagged, running on about two hours of intermittent napping and seven shots of espresso. Give me half an hour of your time, and if by then your answer is still no, Gray Granite will drop the matter for good. You won't ever hear from us again."

*If* it is true. Ainsley would love if it were — but it can't be this good. She knows that if she declines, they will simply find a different location to exploit. Instead of her, different people will make this mistake, people more desperate for the money obviously involved here.

But what can she do? Suffer herself, or let a stranger do it in her place.

Throughout it all, she still sees the person behind this nefarious undertaking — an overworked employee who, under the confident and suave front, is probably crumbling inside.

The least she can offer is a warm drink and her time for her. For Mrs Ingram, not Gray Granite.

"Very well." Ainsley opens the door, checking her wristwatch for her alarm. "Twenty minutes, until the pie is ready. Make it count."

❧

Ainsley has not often seen someone speak so concisely and to the point in her life.

Every moment of those twenty minutes she was given, Mrs. Ingram took and ran with. The rumours were true enough, Gray Granite is interested in building a hydroelectric power station in the region. She has brought maps, blueprints, floor plans, and detailed timelines with expected dates of construction and completion to illustrate this endeavour — and of course, a hefty sum they are willing to part with to pay for the usage of Ainsley's land. She does not dwell on it, but she knows for sure no one in this city has ever even seen a number this big — at least until William is made the same offer, which she is certain they will at some point.

That they have this kind of power is baffling and speaks volumes about Gray Granite's intentions.

Her wristwatch starts beeping then, and just as promised, Mrs. Ingram rises, and thanks Ainsley for her time.

She guides her to the front door, but before Mrs. Ingram leaves into the night, Ainsley has one last question for her.

"And then… What?" Ainsley asks, lifting her gaze from one of the papers she has been handed, and that still litter the coffee table of her living room as they talk outside.

"I beg your pardon?"

"On the hypothetical this power station gets constructed — what happens then?" Ainsley lowers the budget to her side. "To my knowledge, the city isn't exactly in dire need of more electric energy at the moment. Where is this going?"

This is the only question so far that honestly stumps Mrs. Ingram.

"I don't know."

Ainsley raises an eyebrow.

"Even I am not privy to all the details of this project, Ms. Wood. My best guess — off the record, of course — is to sell this surplus to neighbouring provinces, or even countries. Or to future-proof for any booming industries that might need the extra energy. But to be honest?" Mrs. Ingram takes off her glasses, and her eye bags are even more prominent now. "My guess is as good as any."

Ainsley shakes her head, incredulous. Her best guess? Not even the board of CEOs of Gray Granite do know what exactly they are doing there — they are just, well…

betting on an *if*. It is how they started their empire, anyway — why would they change it now?

It all grinds on her gears like sandpaper against skin — but she should have expected it. This is the same Gray Granite that she has heard of all over the news, infamous for their lobbying against land protection laws, indigenous reservations and, yes — deforestation projects galore. Ainsley shouldn't have expected anything different.

What is one more despicable decision under their belt, after all?

"To you, it might just be another construction, another project to show off. But to me?" Ainsley acknowledges the presence of her birch tree behind her, swaying with the wind being carried in and out. "I would feel it all, in my bones. The chaos as every creature flees what once was their home in those woods. The anguish of the earth as the life that cannot run gets flooded. The water would be in my lungs, and I would suffocate forever — until I find a way to live with the constant lack of air, or perish completely."

Mrs. Ingram simply nods as she puts away her reading glasses. "I understand. I will pass your decision on."

Ainsley scoffs. Her mind wanders back to Nangula, and she wonders if her fate is bound to be a repeat of history.

"I do not believe you truly do. You are a witch yourself, your powers come from the same nature that mine do. Are you not at all concerned about your employer's plans? About representing something that goes directly against your own interests?—"

"I am not." No hesitation in her voice, or her steps down the front stairs. " Before anything else, I am a mother, Ms. Wood, and my son can live his dream of attending Harvard because I am able to pay for his education. Moral dilemmas like this are a privilege, and once you prioritise your own, they can come crumbling quite fast — something I am sure you can understand, *elder*." She takes a moment to adjust her glasses. "So I suggest you make your choices, and I will make mine, and I hope we can both go to bed with a clean conscience."

She says nothing else, staring at Ainsley with her piercing eyes and unwavering belief.

All Ainsley can do is stand there, locked into this contest as she pushes her rage down, gripping the door with force. For, despite it all—

Ainsley knows that, much like the dry patches of meadows she encountered earlier today, she is only one. Mrs. Ingram's views won't change.

It's the impasse of the century, and neither will budge.

❧

"Is there a problem here, Ainsley?"

Priscilla, one hand holding desert, the other on her waist, inserts herself between her and this stranger who threatens Ainsley. She poses, making herself as big of a physical barrier as she can to protect her — she has enough experience with Mrs. Ingram's type to do some damage if she wants to.

"Priscilla." Ainsley's demeanour softens instantly as she makes her presence known.

"Do not waste your breath, Ms. Cardoso. My business here is finished." Mrs. Ingram raises a hand to stop this display right there. "If you'll excuse me."

She turns, unceremoniously, and finally leaves.

"What's her deal?" Priscilla asks, still keeping an eye on her, making sure Mrs. Ingram leaves in her car before Priscilla can turn her back on her.

"Nothing good." But Ainsley's mood changes like water to wine upon seeing Priscilla again, her troubled wrinkles gone in an instant. "How much did you hear of that?"

"Most of it, I'm afraid." The draft coming from the mansion had carried most of their conversation. "Who was that?"

"Mrs. Blair Ingram, representing the infamous Gray Granite conglomerate," Ainsley states, her now inky eyes filled with conflicting thoughts.

"Gray Granite!?"

Ainsley nods.

"They wish to purchase my land so they can build a power station over the river."

"What!?"

But Ainsley's wristwatch starts chiming yet again, reminding her of the forgotten dinner in the oven.

"Oh no, the pie!"

Ainsley calls back a vine, getting as much acceleration as she can before jumping, rising and gliding effortlessly over the entire length of her patio. Over the flowers, the foliage, the tables and seats spread out for the festival, leaving only the trailing wave of them behind until she reaches the kitchen.

Priscilla finally sees her, in her element, freely moving as she is accustomed to, and it is — for lack of a better word — magical.

Her mind is still taken aback by the revelation of an offer for Ainsley's beautiful forest — by Gray Granite, of all people — and Priscilla lingers by the Birch on her own hurried stride to the kitchen, doing her best not to ruin dessert as well for them.

She has done her own research about dryads after learning Ainsley was one, trying to get any sort of corroboration on what she has been told. She doesn't expect Ainsley to fit every stereotype or oral story tidbit, but one thing seems painfully true now, as Priscilla stands in this vast building — the birch is Ainsley's soul.

How far do her roots extend? The entirety of the forest surrounding them? The city? Even further still?

Could she feel it when, before knowing anything, she had casually placed that ladybug upon her bark?

What a silly question — of course she had. The thought makes Priscilla's heart twist. She can't even begin to comprehend how that would feel. And now a company wants to build a power station there unaware of the destruction it would inflict on her.

She almost reaches for the Birch again, in curiosity, but retracts her hand before anything is done, choosing to save this question for dinner as well.

Or whatever is left of it to salvage.

<hr>

Ainsley carefully reaches into her oven with towel-shielded hands, and the beautiful Shepherd's pie she had worked so hard on carries the clear signs of a few too minutes past its due, especially on its intricate lacing around the edges.

The burnt smell now permeates the entire kitchen premises with its bitter flavour.

She places the pie on the round table nearby, as it joins the side dishes prepared early and sticks out as the sore loser it is.

What is she supposed to do now? Dinner is ruined.

But through the door, Priscilla joins her, placing the transparent box with her cheesecake side by side with her pie.

"That's not too bad — there should be enough left in the middle there for a good couple of servings. Plus it leaves us with more room for this later on." Priscilla taps the lid of the sweet, and Ainsley chuckles.

"You never fail to see the brighter side of life, Priscilla. It really is commendable."

She smiles, a genuine smile that melts Ainsley's heart and washes away the bad aftertaste of the entire afternoon she had.

But, too soon, it fades from her face as she looks down.

"I'm so sorry, Ainsley — maybe you wouldn't have to have dealt with that woman and Gray Granite if I wasn't so late." She explains herself as if she needs to. "I… I had another episode while getting ready. The apology cheesecake and good vibes are the least I can do to make it up to you."

And, as she expects but struggles to believe still, Ainsley thinks nothing of it. Why would she? Ainsley's heart twists for Priscilla's, that it was hurt so in a way where she suffers from her past still — no matter how far away she is from it all now.

"Please, do not apologise, Priscilla — I know you have no control over them." She places a soft hand on Priscilla's cheek, comforting her, looking with such care at her to make sure she understands. "Instead, I believe you being *fashionably late* a gift. How else would I be able to see you swoop in and so gallantly defend me against Mrs. Ingram?"

Priscilla laughs at the remark and her shoulders visibly relax. Her logical mind knew Ainsley would not mind at all, but her words now finally soothe her emotions.

"Those business types don't scare me, and they sure as hell aren't going to threaten you while I'm around."

Ainsley laughs as well — she wholeheartedly believes her.

They waste no time dwelling on the lost pie or the uncomfortable situation that preceded this, and one by one they carry all the dishes congregated there to the dining room table, displaying them beautifully along the rectangular space.

There is but one tiny problem still.

"Why did you set our plates so far apart?"

As it currently is, Priscilla and Ainsley are sitting on the opposite, shorter ends of this table. It truly looks like a banquet served for a queen and her consort, which apparently also includes them sitting separately. How quaint.

"I did not give it a second thought, to be fair." Ainsley rises from her seat then and brings her chair to the longer edge. Priscilla smiles, promptly following suit so as they sit again, their elbows almost touching.

"Much better, isn't it?"

"Indeed. Shall we commence our feast?" Ainsley makes an exaggerated gesture to the food, and Priscilla giggles.

"Non-ladies first, mademoiselle." She returns a short courtesy in kind.

And so they do.

"Well, do not let me keep you. I am sure there are many questions in your mind, Priscilla. Nothing is off limits — I shall do my best to answer them as best I can." Ainsley is the one to break their silence.

Priscilla ponders over her glass of rosé, twirling it in her hand absent-mindedly. Where to even start?

"Is it true?" She asks. "Can you really feel everything your tree feels?"

That one is still fresh, so she might as well get it out of the way.

Ainsley takes a moment to put the bottle down, but her expression already speaks volumes.

"Yes. It is an interesting, unique experience, one that only I have come to know in this area I think, having that split between body and soul. So you can see why I am wary of anyone tempering with my forest. I know it makes me look like a territorial, greedy overlord, but in truth — I am scared of how it will affect me. Because I know it will."

It already may have.

"Are you the only dryad in the world?"

"Oh dear, no, far from it. But to be fair, for most of my life, I did believe I was the only one. Our existence is a bit isolating that way — the bond to our tree makes it impossible for our earth-walking bodies to stray too far away from it. So, wherever we take roots is where we grow, live, and finally die. It wasn't until the invention of the letter that I was finally able to track down others of us. We may be few, but we are everywhere, each protecting their small corner of this planet since the dawn of time."

But something doesn't quite make sense to Priscilla.

"How can you be so few when you all seem to live for so long? By any means, there should be as many dryads as there are trees." She pauses. "Unless…"

Ainsley does not answer immediately, inspecting one of her forks too intently. She would rather not show her heart so dearly, but Priscilla seems to read her nonetheless.

"Oh… I'm sorry, I should not have asked." She retracts, facing her plate as well.

"Please do not apologise. I meant it when I said you are free to ask anything, Priscilla." Ainsley brings a hand to Priscilla's arm, the lightest touch, lingering, reassuring. "It's true — I am not able to carry children of my own. With our origins being complete mysteries lost to time, conception is not something we have been afforded."

Ainsley stands up then, leaving Priscilla back at the table, puzzled for a moment. She reaches up to a tall bookshelf in the other corner of the living room, lifting a heavy, wide book from it.

She opens it fully as she walks back, browsing her more recent memories and looking for a specific picture.

It's ancient, yellowed by time and bitten at the edges by wear and tear. Ainsley carefully takes it out of the album she holds so dearly with utmost care, and hands it over to Priscilla — who takes it with both hands and delicate fingers — she dares not even breathe wrong around this relic.

And it truly is one.

She recognises Ainsley instantly, her long vines being incredibly short, only ear-length and swept back — although back then Ainsley might not even have gone by 'she'. Wearing a vest and formal shirt with a high neck collar in true Victorian fashion, the eyes that look back at Priscilla are the same ones, framed by the same facial markings that are so iconic to Ainsley.

Side by side, there is this woman that Priscilla has never seen before but has heard about — Eloise, Ainsley's long gone partner, and in her arms, a sleeping Eli. She's a short brunette with uniquely shaped eyes, as if her irises had slitted horizontally, and on her head she proudly wears a set of swirling horns. Eli's are much shorter and stubbier, but they are definitely there on his tiny head as well. The picture is cut at their waist, but Priscilla can already make a good guess that neither mother nor child were human.

"I can finally show you what they looked like, now that you know the truth. We dryads may not be able to bear our own, but we have definitely taken many under our canopies throughout the years. Fostering them, seeing them grow so beautifully." Ainsley looks at the picture as well, with kind eyes and a tightening throat.

"Did…" Priscilla hesitates, but she needs to know. "Did you tell me the truth then, about how they… You know?"

"You mean their untimely death? Yes, unfortunately." Priscilla offers the picture back so Ainsley can place it in the photo album, to keep it safe from the passage of time. "Tuberculosis is a very human disease, which unfortunately affects most magical folk like any other person. Any except me, of course."

Ainsley closes the book, gently placing it to the side for now.

"Such is the irony of life for us. Death, birth, and even illness allude me and my fellow dryads to this day. So I watched Eloise, Eli and so many others perish to an incurable ailment at the time, without being able to do anything but weep at their side, and bury them by the mountain. Which reminds me — I should make the time to visit them this year…"

Ainsley tries to resume her dinner, fork and knife in hand but she stays immovable. The faint light of the candles makes the shadows of her face dance as she whispers the hardest unspoken truth yet —

"… I might be joining them soon."

Priscilla drops her own cutlery now, wondering if she has heard it right. She says nothing, simply looking at the woman she cares for so much with an aching heart.

"Forgive me, I should not have phrased it like so. It might be nothing, but… I should still come clean about it."

"What are you even telling me, Ainsley?" Priscilla is trying to get her bearings, to understand something on top of a truth she has only recently learned about.

Ainsley takes a deep breath, wiping her mouth with a napkin and putting her plate aside.

"How about we have dessert outside?"

⤞ ◦◦◦ ⤝

They sit on a bench on the patio, overlooking the decorated birch tree. By now, they have both finished their desserts in silence — Priscilla does not push as it's clearly something even Ainsley is having a hard time grasping. So she waits.

Their plates with leftover cheesecake lie on a neighbouring bench and they lean on each other as they look up to the stars of the early evening, filtered by the branches up above.

"I… I have told you before that every year, much like my spirit tree, I go into hibernation. Every winter, I sleep, and every spring, I awake once more." Ainsley begins, never taking her eyes away from the stars.

Priscilla nods, resting her head on Ainsley's shoulder, letting her continue.

"That is the truth, and in my aeons of existence, that truth has never failed me once. As soon as the leaves would start falling, I would begin to feel sleep creep up on me, and every winter I would slumber. That sleep, I theorised, is what rejuvenates this body and keeps it from ever ageing or sickening.

But then, one random year, I woke up in spring — two entire weeks too late."

Priscilla lifts her head, failing to see the gravity of the situation just yet.

"I thought nothing of it then, as it had been a particularly bad winter. The snow had melted slower and the flowers had yet to properly sprout. Surely, it was just an anomalous cycle."

Ainsley looks down, resting her head on her hand as she looks at her tree.

"The next year, sleep came earlier by an entire fortnight. And, just as expected, I would wake up in the middle of summer. By then, I already knew something was wrong, but how do you even diagnose a problem such as this? I wrote to all of the other dryads I knew, and for that entire year we debated what could be happening — but still, none of us could come to a perfect conclusion at the time.

Sure — they, too, would perceive small differences in their habitats. Small, expected fluctuations that would grow. Yet their hibernation would be offset by mere days, or hours — if that. I would be the only one to lose that much more precious time.

Ainsley takes a deep breath.

"For a while, things seemed to settle. But it was just the calm before the storm. As the next winter rolled around — that was the scariest year yet — 1984. I could not keep my eyes open and it was just October. As I woke up in spring, for the briefest of moments I thought whatever ailment I was suffering from, I had bounced back to full health. March the 20th, on the dot it was. I was so glad, so chuffed with relief I gathered my bearings and went down the mountain the very next day to spread the good word to everyone — only to find out I was wrong, oh so wrong to have hoped." Ainsley almost slumps now, her ever-present elegance and poise shattered on the floor. "It was the spring of '86, not '85 — An entire year, lost to sleep."

"Oh, Ainsley…" Priscilla wraps her hands around Ainsley's neck, resting her head on Ainsley's back in this hug, as if she could seep the hurt and share its burden.

"At that point, I had given up on the search for an answer. How would I even be able to keep living if I never knew when I would be rejoining this world? How long would it be next? I might as well not make any plans. No more gatherings, no more promises — no more May Day." She sighs, sinking even lower. "And then, I woke up again — on 1987, as if nothing had happened. I was stuck for answers, yet every ounce of information I would receive would only confuse me further."

Priscilla doesn't dare look at the bright side of this — even she knows too much hope can be blinding. Instead, she stays there, a warm embrace to keep Ainsley from sinking to the point of no return.

"Ever since, every winter is a gamble of the dice. Will I wake up next year? No one knows — not even I. Sometimes, against all logic, I will even wake earlier, chilling to the bone in the snow, with no answers in sight. Those years are the toughest. "

Something clicks for Priscilla then, as the pieces fall in place and she sits up.

"That rumour, Ainsley, of this mansion's resident disappearing suddenly, the one that scared everyone in town —" Priscilla cannot believe it. Was it true? That was Ainsley?

Ainsley doesn't answer, but she doesn't have to — her eyes say it all.

Seventeen years. She slept for seventeen long years.

They both sit still for a moment, trying to make any sense of it at all to no avail.

"I am sorry, Priscilla. I am. I tried to explain it away, to hope it away, to promise myself I would wake up perfectly fine next spring as if I had any say on the matter. The truth is, I don't. No matter how much I care for you, it would be downright cruel to rope you into a completely healthy three-month wait alone. But then, it could be another year. Or ten, or twenty, or even —" She can't stomach it, to say the words. Once, she had tried to make her peace with it, praying it would just take her for good and be done with it.

But every time, she wakes, and every time, she finds something worth living for.

In her despair, she barely registers her own confession imbued in the anguish, the bittersweetness of it amidst the chaos of her thoughts. Neither does she realise Priscilla standing up and silently approaching the ribbon-laden tree of her heart.

"Can I?" Priscilla asks, gesturing to it. Her smile is gentle but her lips tremble and her eyes are full of emotion.

She has touched this tree before, as she placed the tiny ladybug upon it, or when they tied the multi-coloured ribbons on its branches — the ones that currently sit around it, bunched up and held carefully until the festival. But now she *knows,* and because she knows, this time it's different. She is not simply reaching for a tree, she is reaching for Ainsley — the other one. The one that, much like the earth-walking one, had refused to be truly vulnerable thus far.

Until Priscilla.

Ainsley stands up too, joining her by the birch. She comes up behind Priscilla, one hand on her waist in an embrace, the other intertwining with the back of Priscilla's own. Ainsley is the one to bring their hands up, gently placing them both upon the bark, hands splayed and overlapping. This close, Priscilla can hear Ainsley's breath hike as contact is made, and how it calms down and evens out as they stay there, connected like that for a moment.

"What can you see, Priscilla?"

But Priscilla sees nothing — her eyes are closed as she listens, and feels.

She expects the bark to be cold to the touch, like any other tree. This is something she had not realised before, but as she tunes into her senses, this tree is almost *warm.* A pleasant warmth, she feels, only a few degrees colder than Ainsley's own hand on the back of hers.

Then, the humming. She doesn't hear it, exactly, but she can sense it, almost like a vibration in the air around them. Faint, oh so faint, but definitely there like the air before a storm comes — hard to describe but so palpable on the hairs of your neck.

In. Out.

Just as Ainsley herself breathes in her ear.

"Do you dream when you hibernate?"

Ainsley expects many questions from Priscilla, but not this one.

"I do. At least… I assume I do. I wake with strange images in my head, sometimes, just as I do when I dream in the warmer months. They are as vague and nonsensical, even more so in the longest ones — but they are definitely there. Sometimes I will even dream of things that I have experienced as a tree — like the sensations of the first ray of sun after a winter storm, or the first bee to land on my flowers as they bloom."

"Hmm." Priscilla almost sings. "Then you're not really gone, are you?

Ainsley reels with this. Of course she isn't — as long as the tree endures, she still lives. But what kind of life is it if she's powerless to enact any change around her?

"Not in a way that matters," Ainsley whispers. "If I am not here next year, who will protect this forest? Who will look out for our own? Who will stop the next conglomerate from levelling this mountain, from demolishing this old mansion to the ground, magical Birch and all to the ground just to build their next monument?"

"We do."

Priscilla is the one guiding them now, as she wraps Ainsley's hand on her waist around her own too, and pulls them forward. Her forehead touches the bark, and all around her, there is Ainsley.

"Me, and Orion, and Estelle, and however many people you have cared for so dearly all these years — and I know they are many. They have relied on you for so much, as I have, and they have trusted you with their lives. And I know it's hard, but you can trust in them too, Ainsley. Even when you can't walk among us any more, we will still be here for you as you have been here for us. We will fight for you, and you can rest for as long as you need."

Ainsley says nothing — not a tear shed, not a cry escaping her closing throat. But she buries her head on Priscilla's shoulder and tightens her hold around her all the same — as the hums around them, calm, now just a constant current in the background.

"Thank you, Priscilla. Oh, you are my first ray of sunshine after a long winter."

She laughs, softly, getting comfortable in this cuddle.

"No need to get sappy on me." She says — but in truth, Priscilla loves it.

They stay like that, interlocked under the moonlight for a moment to be cherished forever, gently swaying back and forth.

To Priscilla, it doesn't matter — her promise from the beginning of this relationship still rings true — if not even more now. She will enjoy every day, every hour and every minute with Ainsley that she can, right here and right now.

Next year she might be here, in this same place and same time — and Priscilla will take her hand and hug her, and kiss her, and make up for the three months away from each other with another May Day festival in tow.

And next year she might be here, moving with the wind as her first leaves appear from the snow, as her flowers sing and grace this earth with another shower of petals and her bark affords her the same comfort her arms do.

Whatever happens, life will go on.

# Chapter 10

"I have one last question for you, but… Ah, never mind. It's silly."

Ainsley and Priscilla have moved back to the kitchen, where each has taken a task for clean up — Priscilla currently washes the dishes on the sink as Ainsley dries them and puts them away.

It's a quiet, domestic intimacy they both enjoy. Dinner for two is always a delight, but sharing the workload of the more boring things in life makes it ever so easy.

Between the clinking and clanking of the delicate china, they have both calmed and settled into this comfortable silence. And in it, Priscilla keeps coming back to that ethereal vision of Ainsley summoning a vine out of thin air and effortlessly gliding over the patio. To Priscilla, she looked downright like a painting of an angel, one barely covered by anything but a piece of sheer fabric, flying in the skies. Oh, what a vision.

But, annoyingly, that is just proof that Orion was right about Ainsley — she *can* control vines, although not the ones on her head... At least not that Priscilla has seen.

God, what is she even thinking?

Ainsley laughs, taking another ornamented porcelain plate from Priscilla's hand and drying it with a towel. "No questions are off the table — even the silly ones. Please, feel free to make them."

Priscilla bites her lower lip in thought, wondering how to phrase it with at least a bit of tact.

"I was just wondering if you could share more about your powers. You were incredible, just flying around on a vine earlier, and well... Can you control other plants as well?"

Ainsley does raise an eyebrow — she has never really thought of her powers as anything to write home about. When others around you can weave magic, breathe underwater, run at super speeds and take the form of powerful animals, being able to tend a garden well doesn't exactly seem groundbreaking in any way. But she indulges Priscilla nevertheless.

"I can, in fact, control any plant life — although controlling someone other than myself takes a much bigger toll on my stamina. It comes especially handy with my backyard garden, as you can imagine, although I don't use it that extensively there. Most times, nature will take care of itself, if you know how to work with it instead of against it. But you surely have realised that facet of my abilities now, no? It has helped you with your work decorating for May Day."

"Oh!" Priscilla had not realised it. "So you *did* create all those flowers outside. I suppose I had a hunch something wasn't adding up with how fast you got it all done — that was a two-day job, minimum."

Ainsley chuckles.

"It's surprising how much can be veiled right in front of someone's eyes. It's how we make our glamours work, even on the less humanoid of folks — if it can be explained away with simple logic, then people usually don't dig much deeper than that. Confirmation bias and such." She sighs. "It is a shame you were not here to witness the creation of your own masterpiece. I had not performed such a feat of magic in a long time before that, and I am quite proud of how it turned out."

"You're right, I would've loved to see that. Gosh, it must have been breathtaking… Thank you for your hard work as well. In my experience, few hosts actually go out of their way to help at all, let alone do something this big."

"There is no need to thank me, my sunshine." Ainsley places a kiss on her temple, putting down her towel for a moment. "Would you like a private demonstration instead?"

"Oh, you don't need to tire yourself out just for me."

Ainsley places herself by Priscilla's side, one arm reaching over her shoulder. The other extends beyond them, to the window sitting right in front of this sink, wide open now and letting a nice breeze come in from the halls.

"For you, Priscilla, I would do so much more."

At the intersection where wall meets window, right at the bottom edge, Ainsley places her hand. Priscilla feels it then, the same hum and magic in the air she had felt earlier on by the birch. The air becomes erratic and charged, and as Ainsley slowly traces that curve, one by one, they sprout — flowers of all shapes and colours, leaves and stems of all sizes, making a beautiful window sill planter with no planter in sight.

"Whoa!" Priscilla's face lights up as it happens and she dries her hands off quickly with her towel as Ainsley finishes bringing life to them.

Priscilla tiptoes to be able to reach them over the sink, but she smells the marigolds and the mint and the nectar flowers — and she melts. All of them are edible too, perfect for a kitchen.

Oh, how delightful this is. Priscilla doesn't even think of the powers other magical folk have — Ainsley is the most powerful of them all in her eyes.

"This is incredible, Ainsley. Thank you for sharing this with me."

Priscilla looks at her again, and Ainsley sees that sparkle once more. Oh, how fortunate she is — to live looking at them forever would be enough.

"That's not all." Ainsley is the one to be a tad bashful now. "Although this facet of my powers has its uses, it can be quite… Unsettling."

Priscilla is curious now.

"I think we're past that point already. C'mon, I can take it."

Ainsley seems to consider this for a moment, but she concedes.

"It will be easier to simply show you as well." She says, turning Priscilla so they can face each other. She brings her hand up to eye-level and Priscilla follows suit.

There, with their palms touching each other, their size difference is quite clear. Priscilla's hands are small and chubby, with dainty fingers and dearly manicured. Ainsley's is almost the opposite — still soft to the touch, but her fingers are long, overtaking Priscilla's by a good inch, with no nails in sight. At the extremities, they are mostly dark like her stripes, with the faint white peeking here and there. Her layers of golden rings are still there, as Ainsley has grown quite fond of adorning herself with them, and they shine in contrast with the polished bark.

But then, slowly and surely, her hand starts to change. Her long fingers shrink and widen, the rings on them struggling to keep up with the shift and rising to the tips to accommodate. A few seconds later — in all but colour and texture — Ainsley's hand is now a perfect replica of Priscilla's.

"You can change yourself as well..." Priscilla says, her mouth open in surprise and wonder. "Are you telling me you can look like anything? Shapeshift?"

"In a way, yes. But the bigger this 'shift' is, the harder it becomes." She brings her hand down, slowly settling back to her old form again. "In my first years walking, I did so by mimicking small bugs at first. At some point, I even tried to fly as a bird, but I found myself too heavy to even lift off. I slowly built up to bigger land animals — this human shape you see now took quite a long time to perfect too, and I still adjust it from time to time to fit my needs. But however similar the shape is, inside I will always be made of bark and sap and vines — my eyes will always look like this as well.”

“No wonder you’re so beautiful…” Priscilla brings her hand up to Ainsley’s face, tracing every angle of her features — her nose, her cheekbones, the arch over her eyes. Ainsley leans into it, eyes slowly blinking and lost in the sensations.

“It’s a poor imitation for a human face — you do not have to lie, Priscilla. Surely a part of you screams in terror as well, however louder your heart wants to talk over it.”

She closes her eyes then, trying to find that little voice inside, screaming in terror of the big bad monster in the dark forest — but all she finds there is affection. Pure, unbridled affection for the spirit of the cairn’s woods. Oh, the twists and turns life throws at you.

“I won’t say it has been easy, getting used to the new appearance.” Priscilla concedes. “But the more I look, the more it grows on me — pun intended.”

Ainsley chuckles.They stay close, interlocked for a moment as Priscilla opens her eyes again to look back at Ainsley.

Those spells are truly something — she can still see the same face she used to know in this Ainsley as well, the same structure and size one-to-one, only now the elevations of the stripes leave a bump as Priscilla keeps tracing in her mental map game. And those eyes, oh, those eyes…

They’re infinite, and Priscilla is right at home in them.

“If you would answer me one question only, in return?” Ainsley requests in a deep breath as she relaxes. She calls herself a ‘poor imitation’ but she melts all the same under Priscilla’s touch — what is fake about that?

“Yeah, of course.”

"What brought your last question on?"

Priscilla freezes, retracting her exploring hand, and Ainsley opens her eyes again, intrigued.

"Far it is from me to question your curiosity or to push you in any way. But I feel you filtered yourself before presenting it to me." Ainsley raises an eyebrow. "What I am saying is, I meant it when I said no questions left unanswered — feel free to leave no stone left unturned, Priscilla."

"Oh, don't mind me, please. It's just something Orion said and it's been stuck in my head ever since — so, you see, it's not even my thought."

Priscilla tries to deflect, for surely it wasn't her thought at first, but it certainly has been hers and hers only ever since — especially before bed last night. Ah, her face burns with it, even now.

"Hmm." Ainsley's eyes are completely open now as she intently studies Priscilla's movements. She did promise not to pry, but she is certainly intrigued by what is getting Priscilla flustered like so — the same Priscilla that had no qualms about asking to touch her literal soul.

Priscilla feels this gaze on her, of course. Well, if she thinks for a second, Ainsley has been around for a while and... The chances of her having been asked the same question before are very likely, aren't they? She's hardly inventing the wheel here.

Right?

She sighs. What the hell.

"He did ask the same question I did, in a way... And technically I have already gotten an answer from you, about your vines."

"My vines." Ainsley brings a hand to her head.

"Yes. The difference here is what he inferred, within the context of the conversation then, of what you could *do* with them, and *where*."

Ainsley takes a moment, perhaps an even longer moment than Priscilla did to get there. Her eyes dart around, one eyebrow furrowed for the longest time.

"And he did, of course, infer to activities in…"

"Bed." Priscilla spurts. "He was referring to the bedroom. Yes. *Activities* in the *bedroom*."

She covers her face in embarrassment, and Ainsley laughs and laughs freely.

"This is what you are so embarrassed to talk about, using my powers for sex." Ainsley has to grab a hold of Priscilla's arm lest she fall back from the embarrassment.

"It's just the cherry on top, you know!? I was asked to be cool with a lot of things all at once, and I thought I was. Until he threw me that curveball and I had to start all over again!"

Ainsley takes a moment to calm herself down from her fit of laughter and offers Priscilla a seat at the kitchen table so they can converse more comfortably.

"I am sorry, I should not have laughed so — but this is so very unlike you, Priscilla. We have shared intimate acts freely already, and thoroughly enjoyed ourselves, have we not? Why be soy coy, all of a sudden?"

"Yeah, of course we did, but this, well — it's just very…" She purses her lips, trying to find the words. "Unorthodox."

"Hmm, I see." Ainsley understands, she does. "But look around you, my sunshine. Our relationship itself is a bit unorthodox, is it not?" What is one more unspoken rule broken of proper, prim society if we are both in accordance?"

Ainsley has a point, of course. She pushes Priscilla's hair behind her ear and places her hand over Priscilla's heart.

"It matters not what others have or will say. What do you desire, Priscilla? My powers are for you to do as you please and you are free to be as creative or comfortable with it as you want — what does that look like, for *you*?"

Priscilla takes a long breath, centring herself and trying to control her heart under Ainsley's warm hand.

She does not have to think for too long, to be honest — these thoughts too have plagued her and she has spent her fair share of time exploring those fantasies in her head as well.

So she joins her own hand with Ainsley's and does her best to describe the images she had conjured up with confidence.

"How many can you work at a time?"

"As many as needed — although we would need to take it slow. I am still fresh from sleep and coordination might be a problem if we don't pace ourselves. So, how many do you desire?"

Priscilla bites her lips in hesitation but finds the courage to mutter it.

"All of them. I… I want to be tied as well."

Ainsley smiles widely.

"Just so we are clear on what that would entail, that includes —"

"Yes, I…" Priscilla clears her throat. "I have my toys at home so you don't need to worry about prep and, well…

There's a bottle of lube in my purse. Is that OK? I don't want to cross any of your boundaries either."

"Of course, Priscilla. But so far it all sounds devilishly delightful. Let me worry about pushing back when I feel it is necessary, yes?"

Priscilla nods.

"Now I have a question for you that you may not have considered before, but that is a possibility if you are willing to entertain it — and even then, it would absolutely be up to you. But would you also be interested in being taken by me?"

Priscilla does not fully grasp what Ainsley is talking about quite yet, thinking she is still on the subject of the vines.

"What I mean by that is, as we have established before, I can reshape parts of my body, which would include —"

"Oh." Oh my God.

It finally clicks — Ainsley can choose what body part she wants, at any time.

"…And you can still feel the same way with either?"

"'The same' would perhaps be pushing it — they are diametrically different experiences. But yes, they are equally pleasurable."

God, her head is going to explode so many times tonight.

"I… I'm not sure. Don't get me wrong, this sounds great but… I haven't had any real experience with anything other than a vulva, or toys. I wouldn't know what to do with it." She stands up now, and walks to the sink. "What I do know is that I need some water, excuse me."

"I understand. I shall keep things as they are then, but if you ever change your mind, know that all you need to do is ask. For now? — Only vines." Ainsley laughs, resting her head on her hand as she props herself against the table and crosses her legs. "Which reminds me — I will gladly take all of you at the same time, but I have one stipulation: that you do not ask to be bound then. If anything goes awry, you would need some way to utter your word or gesticulate for me to stop."

"That's… Really fair." Priscilla agrees, sitting back down with a glass already half empty, but she is almost surprised Ainsley knows what a safe word is.

"Do not look at me so — the magical community invented BDSM." Ainsley chuckles. "This is what I mean when I say 'unorthodox' has no place here. Our powers make scenarios like this commonplace between us as much as good old vanilla — and you too are safe to express it."

Of course. This is the comment that finally soothes Priscilla's nerves for good, and she lets out a sigh she did not know she was holding. She is coming from a place where thoughts like this aren't welcome everywhere. But to them? — and now her as well — this is their 'normal'.

It's fine to want these things.

"So…" Priscilla finally asks, a grin appearing on her face. "Are we doing this now?" There's almost a giddiness in her voice. This conversation alone had worked her up, however matter-of-factly it was, her mind going at a thousand miles with expectation.

"That is completely up to you, Priscilla. The night is still young, and I have no other plans for the rest of this evening than to entertain you. There is tonight's recorded episode that we can watch, and nothing else needs to happen — or I could even take you to your car right now, and we would call it a night."

Ainsley takes the now empty glass from Priscilla and places it to the side. She brings her hand to Priscilla's chin and lifts her head slowly until their gazes lock.

"But if you would rather join me in bed, I will give you everything you have asked me for. That is a promise, my sunshine."

"Ainsley…"

Priscilla closes the space between them with a kiss, bringing Ainsley as close as she can get her.

"There's nothing I would want more."

They tussle and stumble everywhere as they fight their way through the halls, hands and mouths on each other, until they realise they are each pushing to a different side.

"I thought you were taking me to your bed," Priscilla says in between laboured breaths, already working on Ainsley's neck buttons.

"The stairs simply won't do — too slow, especially if I want to keep doing this." Ainsley explains with a grin as she buries more kisses on Priscilla's collarbones.

She pushes them back to the patio instead, on a space wide and open enough to bring forth another vine she can use to leverage both of them up.

But in between the heat and haze of this moment, as Ainsley raises her arm to do so, Priscilla stops her in her tracks.

"Wait. I have a better idea."

She takes Ainsley, holding her hands and slowly walks back, never breaking eye contact. Step by step, through the flower meadow surrounding them and carefully interweaving their path across the strings attached to the ground — until her back is opposite to the birch that started it all, so close.

"Here?" Ainsley asks, pressing her body against Priscilla's and closing the distance between them and the tree with a grin.

"Yeah, here. Is that OK? It's such a wonderful night."

The stars are fully out now, and the faint moonlight tints everything in silver. The silence is only broken by far-away crickets, owls, their own heartbeats, and the ever-present smell of flowers makes this all feel like a dream.

"Oh, Priscilla…"

The way Ainsley pins her against her soul, promptly resuming her touches on Priscilla with a moan, is all the confirmation she needs.

"Ah — But before we start…" Priscilla holds Ainsley by her waist and turns, using the momentum to switch their positions in a blur of hair and leaves. "I want to repay the favour of last time."

Last time, when Ainsley helped her undress.

Priscilla had only seen Ainsley's body with the glamour on her, and since finding out the truth, she has wondered how different the real deal looks under her clothes. Would it be as easy to lose herself in Ainsley's body now as it was then?

Ainsley kisses Priscilla again, and she is acutely aware of how different it feels now — her skin is much firmer on the outside, but still soft and malleable. Her tinted lips are still just as skilled and thoughtful, and she tastes much sweeter now, like raw syrup.

Ainsley breaks their kiss to lay her head back onto the tree, and she almost closes her eyes as she exposes her already half-buttoned neckline to Priscilla.

"I can see the curiosity in your gaze, my sunshine. I'm all yours to explore."

And so she does. Ainsley guides Priscilla's hands to her neck and she locks her in place by hooking a leg behind her thighs. Button by button, down to her chest as it's exposed to the night.

Her hand comes up from Ainsley's thigh, hips, pulling her tunic to reveal her long, thin waist to Priscilla. Then, her chest and shoulders as the garment is shed completely.

Her breasts are still as beautiful as Priscilla remembers them. She brings a hand to one, lightly tracing it with the tip of her fingers — they're firmer as well and any difference in colouration from the rest of her skin to it is a mere suggestion, if that.

Yet, as she brings her lips to its tip, Ainsley lets out the mellowest of sounds in her ear. Oh, how delightful — that is all it takes for any worries to melt away.

She doesn't stop, staying there and enjoying every whimper she can get out of Ainsley, taking pride in being able to break her impeccable poise like so. Under her ministrations, the persona Ainsley works so hard to keep up cracks, and Priscilla can see the real Ainsley shine even brighter.

Priscilla's hand descends from Ainsley's chest, down to her waist. Soon, her underwear is gone as well, joining the pile on the grass. Priscilla doesn't stop, lowering her hand further, tracing every bump on her way down until she finds what she's looking for.

"Ah —" Ainsley lets it escape again between breaths. Her chest rises and lowers as Priscilla peppers kisses on her way down.

Ainsley cups the side of her head as Priscilla looks up. Left only in her knee-length stockings and chunky heels, against the leaves of the canopy and the starry sky, Ainsley is downright a sin to look at. A gift from Earth and The Skies, a feast for the senses and the soul. Immaculate.

Delicious.

Priscilla joins lips to lips and drinks freely — Ainsley is even sweeter there. She moves her tongue back and forth as she finds all the sweet spots that make Ainsley's legs tremble. She arches her back and pushes her hips forward as she moans.

"Priscilla…"

"Yes, Ainsley?"

She looks up, her eyes still full of want. Ainsley holds her face in her hands and brings her up from her knees so she can kiss Priscilla again, lest she continue her explorations to the point of absolutely wrecking Ainsley — she still needs her wits intact if she's to give Priscilla what she wants.

Their tongues intertwine and Ainsley can taste herself in Priscilla. She's now drenched on both ends, but she knows Priscilla must be even worse for wear underneath her clothes.

"Are you quite satisfied with your findings?"

Ainsley asks as she pulls Priscilla closer by her thigh, her other hand on the strings on Priscilla's back, the ones keeping her dress in place. She doesn't quite unravel them, instead tangling her fingers in and searching for skin. Priscilla lets out a long breathy sound.

"Oh, 'satisfied' would be the understatement of the century. You're a wonder of nature, Ainsley. I can't get enough of you and I don't think I ever will."

"But you certainly seem eager to try. Are you ready, my sunshine?"

"Please, Ainsley, I can't wait any more."

Ainsley chuckles, and she is the one to turn their positions again so Priscilla is the one pinned to the tree this time — exactly where she wants her to be.

The vines descend slowly, clinging to the tree and coiling around themselves and the curve of the trunk as the two of them kiss again, gently as it builds with time and expectation. Priscilla moves to untie her dress, but Ainsley intercepts her hands before they can do so, gently lifting them up over her head and holding them, fingers intertwined as the vines grasp Priscilla's wrists and slide down the span of her arms.

"I can undress myself, you know?" But she only teases, comfortably adjusting herself to this new position.

"Priscilla, you are a vision from above, a goddess who deserves nothing less than unending adoration. So lay back, relax, and enjoy yourself. I will take care of everything else."

"Well, when you put it like that…" She gasps as more vines reach her, now around her thighs as they gently pull her off her feet and spread her legs ever so slightly for Ainsley's eyes. "Just promise to be careful, I wouldn't want any tears on it."

"I would not dream of destroying your precious clothes, Priscilla, especially not when they enhance your beauty so. No — but I would like to keep them on, for the show."

"Oh, Ainsley…" Priscilla whimpers with so much affection and care showered on her. More and more vines wrap around her, sliding under her dress to entangle themselves around her waist, her chest, her breasts as they both get cradled. The silky fabric bunches up with the space they take up under there, and an already snug fit leaves much less left to the imagination now.

Ainsley reaches for her breasts too, gently playing with their tips through the fabric, seeing them harden under her indirect touch as little by little, she pulls it down to fully uncover them. Priscilla struggles under the vines' bond, trying to get any sort of relief from the ache in her core against Ainsley's body, but it is to no avail — she is securely tied. The thought does nothing to help her predicament.

"Ainsley, please —" She pleads, but Ainsley brings a thumb over her lips and tuts her.

"You shall have it, my queen. All in due time."

As the vines settle, most of Priscilla's skin is exposed to the night air. Ainsley takes a step back to commit this vision to memory in all its details — the way her smooth skin feels under her touch, her face hot and twisted in desire, her hands gripping Ainsley's vines with her life.

She meant it when she called Priscilla a goddess. Sat on her throne, legs spread and inviting — what else can Ainsley do but kneel in adoration? What else can she do but cover her thighs in kisses and appreciate her already-soaked lacy underwear as she gently tugs it to the side?

"Oh, Priscilla…" She can feel Ainsley's warm breath proclaiming her words against her skin as Ainsley spreads her lips apart and brings her mouth onto her.

Ainsley still feels phenomenal and just like her skin is lined with stripes, so is her tongue. Priscilla cannot contain her voice, her moans joining the symphony of the night in rhythm as she just sits there, bound, feeling every ridge slide in circles against her.

She's still not too far gone not to feel another vine join in — one that had been keeping her waist in place frees itself to slide down her back, under her dress, making twists and turns further and further until —

"Oh —"

"Breathe for me, Priscilla. You're doing so well…"

All Priscilla has been doing is breathing — she's so ready for it.

There's a silent click as Ainsley takes the time to spread the lube around her hand and warm it up. Soon she feels Ainsley's hand coat both herself and the vine that awaits at her entrance.

Ainsley resumes her ministrations at one end as the vine feels its way around the other — sliding over it back and forth and drawing lazy circles around it.

"Ainsley, I can't wait any more, please… I can take it."

"Of course you can. Anything for you, my queen." But her grin is wicked as she looks up at Priscilla to savour her expression as the vine finally makes its way in.

It's slow, excruciatingly so as it feels its way inside her, taking every inch that Priscilla can give. It pulls and gives and little by little it wiggles its way inside fully.

Back and forth, the rhythm picks up, getting faster and faster. The two parts of Ainsley work beautifully together, close and in sync but with just enough syncopation to drive Priscilla mad.

"Oh, Ainsley, it's too much, I think I'm gonna — I'm gonna —"

"Not so soon." Ainsley replaces her mouth with her hand and rises from her adoring bow, slowing down so she can face Priscilla once more. "I promised I would take you completely, did I not? So I am not done with you yet."

Ainsley kisses Priscilla passionately again, keeping the pace with her hand slow as Priscilla feels one of the vines around her thigh unravel and travel up and up before she breaks their kiss.

"Ainsley, please, I… I want you." She begs.

"You have me, Priscilla. All of me."

"No, Ainsley, I mean —" Her eyes, still full of lust, dart down Ainsley's naked body pressed flush against her, down to her hips and back up to lock their gazes together again. "I need *you*."

Ainsley freezes as she understands what Priscilla is truly asking for. She brings a hand to Priscilla's face to carefully lift it by her chin, to look at her with care.

"Priscilla, look at me. I want to make sure this is not a decision made thoughtlessly in the heat of the moment. Are you sure, my sunshine?"

Priscilla takes a moment to breathe and to look Ainsley in the eye with conviction.

"I'm sure." She says confidently. "I still have my safe word. Please, Ainsley? I want us to come together, with you inside me."

Oh, at the state Ainsley is at the moment, it wouldn't take much more — she's just at the brink as well, at the same place she has left Priscilla at. Priscilla was too lost to see, but all this time Ainsley had a vine wrapped around her own leg, playing with herself just enough to keep her hot and bothered for Priscilla.

And the way Priscilla looks at her now, pleading so — she could not say no to her.

She will have what she asks for.

"As you wish, my queen." She relents, and their faces are so close.

At first, Priscilla can only feel Ainsley's hand resume its work and the vine still inside her moves back and forth again, slower now to rebuild momentum.

And then, with Priscilla's core aching, she feels it.

Priscilla expects Ainsley to savour it too, to explore her just as all her vines had — with patience and care. And she does. As Priscilla feels the tip of Ainsley enter her, they moan in unison, mouths agape in between heavy breaths.

What she doesn't expect is for Ainsley to *grow* into her, reshaping herself as she makes her way inside little by little to fill Priscilla up to the brink on every side.

It's so much with every part of her full, every part touched. Priscilla feels so loved.

Ainsley starts to move her hips back and forth, but neither lasts much longer.

"Ainsley —"

"Priscilla —"

Ainsley is the first to come, and Priscilla does too as soon as she feels Ainsley pulsating inside. Waves upon waves of pleasure hit them and Priscilla can feel her focus

slipping as the vines entangled around her torso and arms seem to unravel and relax.

Carefully, while still riding their high, Ainsley brings both of them down to the ground before the entire thing collapses under the strain of the moment. They sit on the grassy floor amongst the flowers, propped against the tree and still connected while catching their breath and gathering their surroundings.

They enjoy this moment in comfortable silence and wish it could go on forever — Ainsley rests her head on Priscilla's shoulder as Priscilla gently caresses her head and lazily kisses her neck. Ainsley's vines are still entangled around her body, but it all lays soft, draping them both in this beautiful mess.

"Ainsley, my perfect Ainsley, my spring flower… Thank you. This night — I'll never forget it." Priscilla hugs her tighter. She really means it too — never was she made to feel like this before, so thoroughly needed. So heard. So loved.

Ainsley musters up just enough energy to hug Priscilla back and let out a content sigh against her neck.

"Anything for you, my summer goddess."

Priscilla too takes a deep breath as she relaxes, before she realises something isn't quite adding up.

"Before I get up to grab us a drink and some wipes, are you —" She hesitates, not knowing if she is misreading her own body or if her inexperience is informing her incorrectly. "Are you still… Hard?"

"Oh, I'm sorry." Ainsley groans at their predicament and immediately apologises. "As you surely know by now, nothing about me is voluntarily soft. A moment, please. Here."

Without the haze and strain of earlier, Priscilla is able to feel that now familiar surge of magic in the air, the same she felt while Ainsley summoned those adorable flowers for her. In an instant, Ainsley retracts herself back to her past form, leaving Priscilla empty of it all except for their mixed arousal.

She accesses the situation and to her surprise finds no actual mess between her legs.

Priscilla chuckles and tries to shove away the thought that if, save both their current lack of stamina, they could very well keep going all night with virtually no refraction time. She stores that information away for now so she can focus on the task at hand.

She gives Ainsley one last, long, affection-filled kiss before detaching herself from their hug of arms and vines.

"Stay here and relax. It's my turn to take care of us."

Ainsley mumbles a complaint, but she takes no action to stop Priscilla from standing up, wobbly legs or not — she'll feel them again tomorrow, she's sure.

For now, a blanket and a drink sound like exactly what they need as well. She may not be able to provide magically enhanced sex like Ainsley, but a nice cuddle and superb aftercare are her speciality.

# Chapter 11

"No, put down the tinsel thread! It's my dress for the festival, not a Christmas tree costume, Orion."

The May Day celebrations will be officially taking place tomorrow afternoon at Ainsley's mansion, and the Moore household is abuzz with preparations on this lovely Friday evening. Priscilla had unearthed this gorgeous pastel pink dress from her wardrobe and thought that, with the right modifications, it would be the perfect piece for her to wear on May Day.

So, why not give it to Orion to tinker away this time? Priscilla might have some basic sewing skills, being the jack-of-all-trades that she is, but Orion does this for a living. However different their personal tastes in fashion are, he owns the machines to make this job much faster.

So she gives him the dress, alongside very specific directions of her vision for this outfit. And he, of course, takes it all and turns it up to an eleven.

Typical Orion.

So here we are, at his corner of the Moore's living room that serves as his personal workspace at home. Priscilla stands on a small step as she wears the aforementioned dress so she is at the right height for Orion to drape this gorgeously embroidered organza around its body.

"Ach, you're a killjoy, Pri. Fine! Now stay still or I'll poke you with this needle." He replaces the shiny thread with a plain one of the same shade as the dress, and gets a few stitches in just to hold things into place.

"Mr. Moore, do something about your son."

Priscilla nags the man, Mr. Adam Moore, as he peacefully sits on a couch a few feet away, watching the local football match on the telly — his trusted cane resting by the arm of the chair. In many ways, Orion and him are mirror images of each other, from the dark hair that now recedes to the eye bags under their eyes. But Mr. Moore sports a much deeper voice and a much warmer personality — Orion's RBF is entirely his own.

"Don't look at me, lassie. We're stuck with him, but you got yourself into this one." He answers with his booming laughter, never taking away his eyes from the match.

"Wait until I'm out of the room to talk shit about me." Orion retorts, but he knows it's all in good fun and even he sports a smile now too. "Turn."

Priscilla obeys, showing him her back so he can continue stitching away.

"I don't even see the problem, Pri — with this dress and the Orion seal of quality I'm putting on it, you'll be the centre of attention in that party. Isn't that what you wanted?"

"That's the exact problem, it doesn't matter what I want — tomorrow is Ainsley's night, so she should be the one everyone turns their attention to, not me."

"What are you even on about? You two are together, Pri, doesn't that make you like… The First Lady of The Cairn or something? You need to hit everyone in the face with your ruffles when you walk in — that's just the rules." Orion lifts her arm so he can reach the seam around her left shoulder and Priscilla sighs. "Besides, I've seen what your love *birch* is wearing tomorrow, and trust me — no one is outshining her."

"How do you know what she's wearing?" Ainsley has kept her outfit for the day a surprise, even from Priscilla, hoping she would dazzle her. That's something Priscilla can respect, but how is Orion getting a peek at this before anyone else?

"Ach, she did try to keep it a secret. But when that Estelle woman came into my shop with a dusty old box, I knew something didn't smell right in Denmark. Then I opened it, and there was this one-of-a-kind gown made of nothing but layers and layers of genuine white muslin? And the cut? I haven't seen it anywhere but in history books. Hell, if I wanted to do my master thesis on that dress alone I could, that thing belongs in a museum and I'm saying that in a nice way."

"Alright, alright, fair." Priscilla concedes, turning again so Orion can work on the other sleeve seam. "This is just a really important day for her, you know? It has to go perfectly."

"Aye, and it will — as long as someone doesn't make a scene on the day because they refuse to catch up with reality," Orion projects his voice in his father's direction.

Clearly, Mr. Moore had not taken the news of magical folk walking amongst his own city very seriously. He mumbles, ignoring the call-out and turning the TV's volume up.

"Are you not joining us tomorrow, Mr. Moore?" Priscilla asks.

"Oh aye, I'll be there — wouldn't miss a chance to get knackered! Hah." He says over the cheer of the stadium over the screen. "But you kids have taken this joke too far now. Fae creatures and ancient magic my arse."

All Priscilla and Orion can do is look at each other and silently laugh.

The room falls into a comfortable silence again, despite Mr. Moore refusing to turn the volume of the game down. Orion sends Priscilla to the bathroom so she can get changed back — now that he has placed the changes down, he needs the dress to finalise everything.

"This reminds me, how was dinner with the woman of the moment?" Orion asks as Priscilla makes her way out and hands him the dress, sitting on a chair by his workstation as he turns on his sewing machine.

She looks around to make sure Mr. Moore is thoroughly consumed by the game, and over the television and the constant hum of Orion's work, she lets herself reminisce about that night.

"I could both kill you and kiss you right now, Orion." She says, and she feels her cheeks grow warm all over again.

"Whoa, *that* good?" He smiles as if he hasn't opened an entire can of worms for Priscilla.

"You were right, you know? She *can* control her vines."

Orion halts, the machine stopping suddenly with him as he gives Priscilla a single clap of excitement and turns on his rotating stool to give her his undivided attention.

"*Do* tell."

"Orion, you're gonna kill me." She buries her face in both her hands before settling with a sigh, head resting on her wrist propped over the sewing table. "It was terrifying just asking her about it, but she was so considerate and composed about it all — and amazing at it, God. I think that night changed me for good, Orion, and it's all your fault for even putting the idea in my head. How can I ever have vanilla sex ever again?"

Priscilla pretend-fights him, throwing punches against his arm and he shields himself between giggles.

"Ouch, watch it, watch it, you're stronger than you look, you sexual heathen —" The sarcasm in his voice is clear as he fights back. "You're welcome, by the way."

"Oh, you might change your mind about that, Orion… Wait until I tell you the rest."

"What?" He raises his eyebrows in clear confusion.

"The vines aren't everything she can do. Oh, how do I even put it? Um." Priscilla brings her index to poke her cheek in thought. "Let's say she has some limited… *Shapeshifting* powers as well."

"Aye, aye, the magical tree can shapeshift as well. That's just grand." He barely gives it a thought, to be honest.

After the talking, walking tree spirit, witches, fairies, and whatever else out there, what's one more power to add to the list? "Hold on —"

"Yes." She elaborates no further, simply choosing to mimic the rather unusual act with her hand — a fist at first, slowly unfurling her fingers upwards.

Orion says nothing, choosing instead to drop his head forehead first onto his sewing table, the only thing cushioning and muffling the very clear 'thud' it makes being the dress halfway done.

Priscilla pities him, she does. First, Cass's ex reportedly possessing two, now Priscilla's current engagement having the ability to pick willy nilly what suits her fancy at the moment.

"Fuck me." He proclaims, his face still smushed by fabric and table, and Priscilla pets his back.

"There there. It will be OK."

"It better fucking be! What's the good of us poor humans having science if I can't even use it to one-up the magical twats in the dick-measuring contest!? Five years I've been waiting, Pri, five years — and no dick in sight!"

She tries to contain herself, she truly does, but the absurdity of this conversation is too much and she lets a laugh escape.

"Orion!"

"What!?"

She grabs him by the shoulders to lift him up, and his already exhausted face looks even worse for wear with the pressure marks of the fabric folds imprinted onto his forehead.

"Help me out for a change, will ya, Pri? If I storm the Parliament and demand those pricks give me, at least, a dick and a half by the end of the year — will you be there for me?"

She snorts, but his plea is half-ground in reality, she can tell.

"I'll be right behind you with the pitchforks and torches. I promise."

Satisfied with her response, he gives her a sad thumbs up before resuming his work on her dress.

Orion works fast, but even his skilled hands cannot perform any miracles. Priscilla eventually settles for watching the match on the TV as well, despite knowing next to nothing about the sport.

It isn't long until the peace is disturbed, however, as an energetic Cass blasts the front door open, a young girl in toe — the youngest of the Moores, eight-year-old Lucy.

With a full backpack on her, fresh out of her school day and ready for the weekend, her dark pigtails bounce from side to side in excitement as she sees Priscilla and the rest of her family.

"Pri, Pri, Pri! Are you here to watch cartoons with me?" She throws her bag to the side and jumps on the sofa, the controller already in hand.

"Lucy!" Priscilla chooses violence instead, viciously attacking the girl with a flurry of tickles. "Let your father finish the game first — but of course. Bingo Bongo again?"

"Bingo Bongo! Yay!" She giggles, comfortably settling on the couch by Priscilla's side.

"Oh, it's a family gathering, is it?" Cass carefully places her motorcycle helmet and keys on the table by the hall, joining everyone with a smile. "Alright, it's the end of the month and we've no decent food 'till payday, so who's cashing out for dinner this week?"

'Not me.' They say one by one, even young Lucy joining the game. Priscilla is the only one to miss her cue — her phone rings, and her response to it is instant.

"Ainsley? Is everything alright?"

The entire room quiets to listen to the conversation.

"Who's that?" Lucy asks her father.

"Priscilla's new girlfriend."

"That's the dryad we were talking about, Lucy." Orion chimes in.

"The tree woman!? Cool!" The girl exclaims, unaware of her volume.

"Oh, that's Lucy, Orion's younger sister," Priscilla explains as she ruffles Lucy's hair for interrupting. "Yeah, Orion is giving me a hand with my dress for tomorrow, so I'll be at his place until he's done."

Priscilla covers her phone to explain the situation to an already distracted Orion.

"The rehearsal is driving her crazy, she wants a reason to bail early. So, since I'm already paying for dinner, apparently — would it be OK to invite her over?"

There's a clear look of delighted surprise between Cass and Orion, and Mr. Moore's booming laugh seals the deal.

"Time to meet the in-laws."

"Tree woman!"

It takes Ainsley a very short time to find the Moore household as it currently lies incredibly close to the current bounds of the city and her forest. It would have been a shorter walk still if she had a trail to follow down the mountain, but as it is, she's quite happy to take the shortcut through the thicker parts of the woods.

She emerges on what looks like a park for the local younglings — an open grassy area with swings and climbing bars. It's a simple residential neighbourhood with identical houses lined up across the streets, and the one she's looking for is but a few blocks away.

It's a two-story in red brick and dark roofing, and the garden lays bare except for the front entrance covered in grass and children's toys. In the garage, Orion's car and Cass's motorcycle share the open space, almost blocking the short fence's gate.

Ainsley knocks on the door, and an excited Lucy is the one to answer.

"Whoa! *Giant* tree lady!" She exclaims as the door opens and Lucy stands there in awe.

"Lucy!" Cass berates her from inside.

Ainsley laughs and crouches down to eye level with the girl.

"A pleasure to meet you — Lucy, was it?" Lucy nods as Ainsley points to herself. "I'm Ainsley. Would you mind showing me the way in?"

So Lucy skips and hops a few steps, showing Ainsley the living room after a brief time in the entrance hall.

It's a pleasant interior as well, with bright walls, wooden floors and mixed bits and bobs spread out throughout a surprisingly big living space, each giving a glimpse into each resident's life — a sewing workspace on the back, a Rangers flag by the ornamental fireplace, a couple of motorcycle helmets on multiple surfaces and boxes upon boxes of toys on shelves by the wall-mounted television.

It's a home, full of life and personality, and Ainsley feels the warm welcome of the Moore household as soon as she ducks through that threshold.

One by one, Orion introduces his family members, from oldest to youngest — Mr. Adam Moore, father and head of the house, who apologises for not standing — 'Bad knee, you see.'; Cassandra Moore, the oldest of his children and the firmest handshake of them all; and young Lucy Moore, who has already receded to her afternoon cartoons and only offers a wave and a grunt.

Ainsley sees what Priscilla means by how she has found her place with the Moore household — it's a loving family, something she must have found great comfort in after fleeing her biological relations, no doubt. Which brings us to the question —

"Where is Priscilla currently? I was under the impression she was already present before my arrival."

"We're doing some last-minute alterations to her dress for the festival tomorrow. She should be out any second now." Orion explains.

As if on cue, Priscilla descends from the stairs, sporting the aforementioned dress in all its glory after all the requested alterations. The peach-pink of the fabric compliments her hair perfectly as it trails behind her, the many beads and sequins line the silhouette of the corset bodice in a pattern of different arabesques, all glittering as she turns. The sleeves are of the same material as the skirt, a simple layered ruffle that leaves most of her arms and shoulders free to move. Her twists are tied up in a bun, one or two strands falling off to the side and perfectly framing her face.

"Ainsley, you're here!" Priscilla notices her, and her smile could brighten up the world. She practically hops down the remainder of the stairs to greet Ainsley with a kiss and a hug.

"Have you met everyone already?" She asks.

"Indeed I have — Orion was kind enough to handle the introductions while you were away."

Priscilla nods and, still hooked to Ainsley's neck, notices her human form is the one to smile back at her.

"Oh, there's no need to keep up appearances here, Ainsley — I've told them."

Of course, to make the trek here, Ainsley still wears her glamouring earring so as not to draw any curious eyes throughout the neighbourhood — and Mr. Moore makes sure to point out her perfectly usual physique, in spite of her unique height.

"What, is your dear Ainsley going to transform into a tree spirit now? No offence, but that's something I'd like to see with my own eyes." Mr. Moore adds from his place on the sofa couch, leaning forward to get a better look through the crowd around her.

"Stop being a bugger, dad. You'll be eating your words soon enough." Orion intervenes.

"Are you sure?" Ainsley has to double-check — her last time revealing herself to Priscilla alone was tense enough. A room full of people, especially one with individuals that are already averse to the idea? That is tantamount to disaster.

But a bright-eyed Lucy looks expectantly at Ainsley, not saying what she wants in case Cass finds it improper, but saying it nonetheless as she approaches her.

These folks are Priscilla's family, the people who took her in at her lowest and gave her the possibility of a future, and all the love she had never had — Ainsley needs to believe in their ability to accept her truth as well.

So she reaches for the earring that conceals her true form, and just as she had revealed herself to Priscilla, she does to the Moore household — right here, right now, on this Friday evening.

The room falls silent save pointed gasps as the illusion cascades off Ainsley's figure, hair turned to leaves and skin to bark in a few seconds. As she opens her eyes once more and they look back to the family she performs an exaggerated bow.

"Let me reintroduce myself — I am Ainsley, the birch spirit and guardian of the Cairn you have so dearly called your home's backyard — and it is my pleasure to remake your acquaintance."

"Tree lady!" Lucy exclaims once more.

"Jesus Christ on a wheelbarrow…" Mr. Moore jumps from his seat, bad knee be damned to get a proper look at the dryad standing in his living room. "So it's true? No pranks, no tall tales?"

"I would not lie to you, Mr. Moore." Ainsley extends a hand as he takes laboured steps towards her. "It is a pleasure."

He hesitates for a moment, looking Ainsley up and down with a worried frown. But he also sees the way

Priscilla leans ever so slightly towards Ainsley, an air of familiarity to be in each other's space like so.

They're together — and for Mr. Adam Moore, this is reason enough.

"The pleasure is all mine, lassie." He takes her hand with a strong handshake and a laugh from the chest. "Now for the real question! Whisky or Lager?"

The two oldest groan in second-hand embarrassment, throwing hands in the air — leave it to Pa to get anyone that has been through the door for longer than a quarter hour drunk. You might say it's his love language.

It's that simple, really, and after they exchange their drink preferences and talk for a while before dinner arrives, the biggest rift that divides Ainsley and the Moore household is that she is somewhat of a Celtic fan.

❦

It's a lovely night-but-not-quite as Priscilla and Ainsley make their way to Priscilla's flat on foot, hand in hand as they take their time on a lovely stroll.

It is night-but-not-quite because, despite the clock on both Priscilla's phone and Ainsley's wristwatch pointing to a full nine hours in the evening, the sun has barely begun to set in the horizon, its presence being still felt thoroughly even behind the clouds.

They talk about anything and everything really, but Priscilla takes special interest in the stories Ainsley has to tell about her past with drinking, especially at the local pubs.

"I will tell you this now and I will stand by it for the rest of my days — there is nothing like taking the very sinuous, very long trek back up the mountain when you are so drunk you cannot reliably tell your left from your right — especially when you are so unaware of yourself that you've lost your glamour somewhere halfway through there."

"No way!" Priscilla bellows out a laugh and it barely reverberates over the sound of the cars passing by. "How many urban legends do you think you started just by making your way home all drunk like that?"

"Too many to count." Ainsley joins the chorus. "You must be fair here, however — when you have lived as long as I have, the amount of mistakes one has committed will add up to a glorious mess much easier."

The conversation on the rest of the way is light-hearted still, and they laugh freely as it is their right in this forsaken existence, drunkard tales and all.

But as the heat of the day starts to take its toll, and so very close to their destination as well, Priscilla sees the once joyful Ainsley suddenly quiet down. Her eyelids seem heavier, and her breathing is almost erratic.

"Ainsley, are you OK?" At first, Priscilla almost thinks she's just re-enacting her days of cryptic behaviour, but when her knees buckle and she seems to tip on nothing but air, Priscilla begins to worry.

"I — I am fine, simply a tad light-headed." Ainsley lets herself lean on Priscilla for support on the last few feet until their destination.

Priscilla thinks nothing much of it — the day is really warm and she feels a bit light-headed herself, and Ainsley seems to recuperate quickly anyway.

But inside Ainsley is the one having a fit of panic. However calm her exterior seems to be, Ainsley is no mere human and changes to her body — especially ones that seem to sap her energy out of nothing — can only mean trouble.

She knows it does. But she looks at the woman in front of her, enjoying the small pleasure of a slow evening walk with her…

She knows. But she loves Priscilla too much to burden her more than she already has. Ainsley has to tell herself it will be alright.

As they finally reach the flat, Priscilla insists Ainsley lay down on her bed and she hopes the small floor fan she turns on will do its job and cool both of them down. There is a nice breeze coming in from the window as well, and the fabric dappled over the canopy of the bed flutters back and forth, in and out of Ainsley's vision as she looks up to the ceiling of Priscilla's bedroom.

She joins her too, and side by side on the double bed, they laze the rest of the sunlight time away. It's a long cuddle so they can rest and digest the wonderful dinner they had had, and enjoy the slower moments of life.

"Are you nervous for tomorrow?" Priscilla asks, laying her head down on Ainsley's chest and feeling it rise and lower with her breathing. There is no heartbeat at all, and it is almost surreal to experience this closeness and warmth without the rhythm of a heart inside.

"I am not." She says matter-of-factly.

"Really?" Priscilla looks up to meet her eyes.

"I will be amongst friends and family, both old —" Ainsley places a chaste kiss on Priscilla's forehead. "And new. What is there to fear?"

"Well, when you put it like that…" Priscilla concedes.

"Are you, my sunshine?"

"Me? Why would little old me be nervous? I'm just a guest."

"A guest that has worked tirelessly to make this festival a reality. I imagine you are not often invited to events for which you have poured your soul into, do you?"

"Oh, that's the crucial part right there — I've been invited to a few, but the ones I truly envied the guests for are very few. One or two weddings I was lucky enough to be asked to help, and maybe one Princess-themed birthday party, once. But those I've only really got to see in photos the day after. Everything else? Simply not worth bending myself for."

"Did you not enjoy those other assignments?"

"It's a job, just like any other, Ainsley. I'd love to do nothing but lavish weddings and unique quinceaneras and fun festivals for unique persons, but there's a lot of money in rehashing the same colour palette for any other company." She shrugs. "One day we might change things enough so that I don't have to use my passion as my source of income. But today is not that day."

"I am sorry to hear so. Know that if it were within my grasp, I would change the world. For you, and me, and all of us."

"Oh, don't say things like that, Ainsley." Priscilla wraps her arms around her and holds her tight as if her presence were to scare all her worries away. "If a literal immortal being with nature superpowers feels powerless against it all, then what am I supposed to do? It's hard enough as it is."

Ainsley turns them both on the bed so they are both on their sides at face level, looking at each other.

"You do what you have always excelled at — taking care of each other, through thick and thin. You may not have the powers, but you have the numbers, and you personally know how much stronger having the support of people you know and care about is important. Not only does it make you stronger as a collective, but look at yourself, Priscilla."

Ainsley brings their foreheads together and they can feel each other's joy emanate from their connection.

"You aren't just my sunshine — look at how much joy you have brought everyone else around you too. You are the first ray to grace their lives after a long storm. You should find both pride and strength in that."

"Ainsley..."

The kiss that they share then means so much more than simply two people coming together — it is so much bigger than just them. Yet they are oblivious, for all they need is the love they have for each other, so it can grow and overflow and spread everywhere on this Earth.

Let it be.

# Chapter 12

Lazy kisses turn into lazy hands on a lazy Friday evening. Priscilla takes Ainsley's bout of fainting earlier on seriously and lets her rest for as long as she needs, but lazy kisses turn into intentional hands turn into a passionate Friday evening. Priscilla remains on top, legs spread over Ainsley's body as she brings sloppy lips to every inch of skin she can find — up the arms, over the slit of chest of her deep v-neck under her blazer, around her neck and on every centimetre of her face. Every kiss a mark in shiny bergamot-scented lipstick, leaving smudged dots of affection everywhere they have been, concentrated around Ainsley's own mouth as it hangs open.

Under Priscilla's careful touches, Ainsley now lays deliciously dishevelled and properly out of breath — in a good way now. A thought that, despite feeling her own desire build as she looks down at Ainsley, keeps her from going any further.

"This is lovely, but we should be taking it easy and cooling down, not getting even more heated," Priscilla says as she hovers over Ainsley by barely an inch, her breath tickling Ainsley's neck and sending shivers down her skin.

"It was a momentary setback, my sunshine, I assure you. Night draws in and I feel much better now — more than better, if I might add." She grins, looking up at Priscilla. Clearly, the position is doing something for her by the way she grips Priscilla's thighs — a detail that does not escape her attention.

"Oh, really?" Priscilla hums, rolling her hips forward and grinding over Ainsley to test the waters.

Her experiment pays off as Ainsley digs her hands even deeper into them, letting out a raspy breath for her.

"You gave me the night of my dreams, but I never asked you what your preferences are, Ainsley, did I?" Priscilla notes.

"You are very well aware of my preferences, my sunshine — soft brown skin with delectable citrus-flavoured lips and deep rounded eyes that look back at me with such want... Oh, I have been blessed tonight for I lay snugly locked in between the legs of my wildest winter dreams."

Priscilla feels the heat rise to her cheeks at such a heartfelt compliment, however lust-drunk Ainsley is as she professes it. She almost wants to feel coy for it, but Ainsley finds as much purchase as she can under Priscilla's body to push against her hips in search of that same high, breaking whatever insecurity might hover over her head.

"C'mon, Ainsley, you can only distract me with your pretty words for so long. You can tell me what you want or I can just keep you right here under me, all night long." Priscilla rocks her hips once more and it elicits an even stronger reaction from Ainsley. "Unless…?"

Bit by bit Priscilla picks up the cues Ainsley so generously gives her, making up the puzzle as they go. Ainsley rests one of her arms on her forehead, shielding herself from Priscilla's gaze as she looks almost embarrassed to be the one under scrutiny for a change.

"Unless being under me like this all night long as I have my fun with you is exactly what you want, Ainsley."

Ainsley shakes her head, not in disagreement, but in utter disbelief.

"And I assumed my resolve unbreakable — yet here we are. You can read my every thought and intention, my sunshine. How do you do it?"

"It's not that hard." Not when she is responding so well to Priscilla. She smiles, placing a chaste kiss on Ainsley's lips as she lifts Ainsley's arm from where it rests. "I don't mind being more dominant, Ainsley. You know, I might even get a taste for it when the view from up here is so pretty."

Ainsley brings her hand to Priscilla's face, tracing the upper line of her smudged lips as their colour compliments the marks on her skin so well.

"Oh, Priscilla… You have submitted so beautifully to me that the possibility had never even crossed my mind. But you have caught me, and I do not believe I can deny it any more. If you will have me tonight, I am yours to do as you please."

This stirs something in Priscilla she did not know was there — this need to see every one of Ainsley's needs and pleads satisfied, but in this new light now — a barrage of pleasure brought by her own two hands this time.

Oh, what a thrill. But she takes a deep, shuddering breath to contain herself, to talk with a clearer mind.

Just as Ainsley had taken the time to ask the questions and set the scene for her yesterday, Priscilla is the one to do so tonight — pushing for boundaries and setting her own in turn, asking for her pleas and making plans together, leaving just enough detail left for the imagination.

And that is how Ainsley finds herself standing in front of a long wall mirror, one sitting in between drawers and a vanity table by the corner of the room. The last rays of the day filtered through the curtains mix with the fairy lights lining the walls and it all makes her white skin glow. She takes her last article of clothing off, folding it neatly and placing it over the drawer wardrobe by the small fan. As she turns to look back at herself, her vines flutter with the wind the fan brings in from the window as Priscilla finally joins her.

Priscilla had taken the time to change herself into more appropriate clothes — a silky night dress that leaves just enough covered for the mind to wander. The juxtaposition of her bare, naked body against Priscilla's covered one — however little — adds to the tension she already feels polling in her lower stomach.

"Nervous?" Priscilla asks, placing the last of her toys on the vanity table, and lining them up on a piece of cloth.

"Not at all. I trust you, Priscilla — all I feel is desire." Short, sweet, confident. Ainsley is ready.

Priscilla wishes she could say the same. This is new territory for her, and however much she wants this too, wanting can only achieve so much — she needs to do it now.

But as she stands there, side by side with Ainsley as they both look at their reflections under this soft, ethereal light — Ainsley looks incredible.

And tonight, she's in Priscilla's hands. She will make it memorable, for both of them.

"Enlighten me, my sunshine. What do you wish me to do first?" Ainsley asks expectantly, but never takes her eyes away from Priscilla's reflection.

Priscilla offers no verbal command at first, simply reaching into the stash of assorted items she had collected for the night and producing from it a yarn of satin ribbons.

"Right now? You'll just stand there, looking pretty for me while I doll you up." No question or option — a simple command as she smiles dreamily at her.

Ainsley obeys and stays perfectly still, only observing Priscilla's movements through the mirror and feeling her position Ainsley's arms crossed behind her back. It's a euphemism, really, 'dolling her up' — what Priscilla is truly doing is tying Ainsley's hands very securely behind her back, twisting the ribbon around her arms and tying them in neat bows at the sides.

She doesn't stop there, however. Within a few minutes, Ainsley's entire torso is wrapped in the shiny string in an intricate pattern of knots and interlocking lines. The soft green of it pops in-between her stripes and lipstick marks in a deliciously constricting picture that she watches unfurl right in front of her eyes.

"How does it feel?" Priscilla asks as she assesses her own work, pulling the ribbons tighter with a small tug.

"Snug, yet comfortable. To be in the presence of your work is already an experience on its own, Priscilla, but I am sure I am one of the few that has the honour of being enwrapped in it — quite literally."

Priscilla smiles with pride.

"Good. But I'm not done yet."

Priscilla gives Ainsley one last tug around her waist before reaching into her vanity table once more. From it, she searches her collection for one of the more mundane pieces in it — a simple pearl necklace.

"Have I not seen you wearing this same accessory before?" Ainsley asks, knowing this to be one of Priscilla's staples in her wardrobe.

But she shakes her head with a devious grin. "It wasn't this one, that's for sure. This chain doesn't go around the neck."

Ainsley raises an eyebrow as Priscilla comes forward, untangling the beads and pulling it taunt to test its strength.

"Then... Where?" Ainsley asks, genuinely curious.

Priscilla chuckles. "You'll see."

That is all Priscilla offers, but Ainsley does not have to wait too long to understand. Priscilla comes in between her and her reflection to tie one end of the chain to the ribbons keeping her bound, hooking one of the clasps to the flat green string knotted right over what would be her belly button. For a moment she assumes this will be just another layer of adornment around her waist, but as Priscilla's hand guides the chain down instead of to either side, Ainsley becomes very aware of the practical use for these pearls.

Down, tight in between her lips and cheeks, the other end hooked to a knot over the small of her back. The smooth texture makes the pearls slide easily, back and forth and rolling from side to side, the coolness of them an added layer to Ainsley's awareness of how they fit around her sensitive spots.

"Oh." Ainsley gasps at the contact, and then again as Priscilla pulls on it to adjust the length.

"Well? How does it feel?"

"It's… perfect. When you mentioned you would be adorning my body, I did not expect anything other than just a treat for the eyes. Suffice to say I am impressed by how practical it also seems to be."

Priscilla giggles. "It should give you something nice to enjoy while you take care of me."

"Your turn, my Queen?"

"Yes, but not so fast — there's one last detail missing."

Priscilla takes a moment to trace a feathery touch over Ainsley's mouth as she inspects the mess she had left there. The lipstick is dry now, spread everywhere on her face with not nearly enough left over her lips for her liking. So she rummages through her vanity once more, quickly finding another one of her favourite shades — a deep, glossy red.

She uncaps the intricate packaging, rolling it up to reveal her plans to Ainsley and they both smile in agreement.

They'll match.

Priscilla brings the stick to Ainsley's lips, depositing a generous amount of the shiny material on her as Ainsley keeps her mouth slightly agape. She doesn't bother getting the shape perfect, but the scent of cherries mixes with the orange already in the air, a preview of moments to come. Ainsley's eyes fixated on Priscilla's throughout it all, her gaze full of desire.

"It suits you," Priscilla notes, putting the tube back down on the table, returning her hungry gaze to Ainsley's.

"It will suit you better."

Ainsley doesn't wait for a command to bring her mouth to Priscilla's, promptly smearing it everywhere in return and pinning her over the mirror with her body weight. Priscilla hooks her fingers around the ribbons over Ainsley's chest to control her movements. First to pace their kiss — passionate, tongues tracing over lips and making an even bigger mess now, red and orange combining into a completely new colour. Secondly, to slowly bring Ainsley down to her knees — Ainsley's mouth never leaving Priscilla's body on her way, marking every single expanse of skin she can get over and under her gown.

Priscilla transfers her grasp to Ainsley's chin, then to the back of her neck to appreciate the view of Ainsley looking up at her from different angles. Ainsley feels Priscilla's gaze on her, enjoying a job well done by both parties. She strokes Ainsley's cheeks, making sure she is ready for what she will ask for next.

"You missed a spot." Priscilla teases, bringing one of her legs over Ainsley's shoulder.

"I'm sorry, my Queen. Let me make this right."

Ainsley leaves a kiss on Priscilla's palm before diving right in, plunging herself into her lover with vigour, lapping over her entirety before showering the area with cherry-scented, sloppy kisses. Over her thighs, her stomach, her lips, everywhere she can reach at this level to later return to her clit, circling it slowly and drawing sweet, sweet sounds from Priscilla's mouth.

Priscilla takes Ainsley's head with her hand, combing her vines back to keep them out of the way as she pushes her hips closer to Ainsley's mouth.

"Oh, Ainsley, yes. Keep doing that, it feels so good…"

The praise encourages her further, and the push and pull of Priscilla's hips move the pearls tied to her back and forth as well, driving her mad with desire.

So she doesn't stop, slowly building up a rhythm with Priscilla, moving with her. She only breaks it to get further in, to tease at her entrance with the tip of her tongue only to move back to her clit again later. Priscilla moans even louder now and oh, it is music to Ainsley's ears — she can feel her own arousal drip down her legs.

Priscilla's grasp on her head tightens. On the side of her vision, she sees Priscilla's free hand reach out for another item over the desk, searching for a good moment as she's too distracted to look for it — a plug made of very reflective glass, transparent and leaving a trail of rainbow specs across her vision as the light hits it, already lathered in lubrication.

Ainsley follows it as Priscilla brings the toy to her back, and she pauses for a split moment, just enough to get a good look at Priscilla pulling and pushing it inside.

"I'm so close, Ainsley — don't stop."

She doesn't need to, putting her mouth right back at work. Her arms may be tied at her back, but that won't stop her from helping out as she can — and she can do much more.

She calls on the vines pulled over her back, and a couple of them move around the two, sliding their way up Priscilla's legs as she gasps in surprise until she realizes what's happening. The vines coil around her cheeks tightly, pulling them apart to ease the plug's entrance, and Priscilla moans as it slips in fully.

Her hand goes right back to Ainsley's head, and she takes this chance to shove her tongue inside Priscilla, feeling the shape of the plug through the thin wall keeping them separate.

"Oh, Ainsley —"

Priscilla doesn't get a chance to continue. She comes and Ainsley can feel every contraction in her mouth — once, twice, until Priscilla is nothing but a puddle of pleasure over her. She drinks every drop, enjoying the show from below as Priscilla's hips slowly still.

Ainsley finally comes up for air, letting her vines go and looking up at Priscilla, her eyes full of devotion. "Was that satisfactory, my Queen?"

Priscilla grabs her by the chin again, pulling her up to eye level and kissing her passionately — citrus and cherries but mostly her own taste in it.

"Very. But it looks like I need to tie your vines down too, huh?" Priscilla says, still breathless and coming down from her haze. Ainsley smiles.

In a moment, Priscilla twists, changing their positions with a delighted sigh so she faces Ainsley's back now. She gently pushes her forward, and Ainsley is the one to feel the cold sting of the mirror against her bare chest and face. She hisses at the contact.

She feels Priscilla's hands gather all of her vines behind her into another secure ribbon knot, a low ponytail that lightly pulls her head back. What she doesn't expect Priscilla to do is to tie her ponytail to the same ribbon holding the pearls around her. What a perfectly impossible predicament — every time Ainsley tries to push her head back down to look at anything but Priscilla over her shoulder, or if she even tries to move one of her vines free, it will push the pearls against her even tighter.

"Oh, you are positively devilish, Priscilla," Ainsley says in between a moan as she shifts to get comfortable, looking over her shoulder to her captor. Her love.

"But I'm not even done." She says primly, but her eyes speak another truth.

Priscilla kisses Ainsley's back, peppering her skin with more kisses. Ainsley cannot see it, but from the way Priscilla moves, she knows Priscilla is putting the rest of her toys in motion. And if memory serves her right, the only thing left there is —

She feels a silky smooth object brush against her thighs, setting itself in the gap between them, hovering right under her lips as they coat it with her own arousal.

"Ah — is that…?"

Priscilla finally settles behind her with a whimper, her breasts and face touching Ainsley as Priscilla holds her hips firmly with both hands.

"The strap-on, yes. You promised me a night to do whatever I want with you, my Ainsley, my summer blossom — and I'm holding you to that promise." Ainsley feels Priscilla's hand bring her tights together around it to

slowly rock Ainsley's hips back and forward, completely covering the toy with her dripping fluids.

The friction this movement brings as it clashes against the chain of pearls still tied around her is torture, pure torture, and she moans freely for Priscilla to hear.

"Priscilla, oh — Please —" She begs between belated breaths.

"Keep saying my name like that, Ainsley."

She pushes the chain to the side and lines the toy up with Ainsley's entrance before bringing their hips completely together in one sweeping motion.

It's almost enough. Almost. But Priscilla locks their hips together tightly, not giving any wiggle room for Ainsley to move to chase release, no matter how close to it she is.

She feels Priscilla's hand reach around her waist, sliding her hand down to her lips. Her other slides in between them. Ainsley hears the faintest click and the toy connecting them comes alive.

"Priscilla —"

"Ainsley —"

Priscilla finally moves them with slow, languid strokes, and with all of this care, as she's encased by Priscilla's touches, she comes. Her moans reverberate in her chest for Priscilla to feel as she holds her up, her knees faltering in the overwhelming pleasure of that moment.

She barely registers it, still feeling the bliss of her high as Priscilla pulls out and brings them both back to bed, leaving the toy off and behind at the vanity table.

"Oh, my Queen —" Ainsley tries to catch her breath as she's lowered onto the sheets. Priscilla straddles her again, just like she did earlier to entice them into their current situation. But now her kisses are chaste as she whispers against Ainsley's collarbone, slowly but surely undoing the many knots that keep her tied.

"Beautiful. So beautiful…"

Ainsley only has the strength to display a blissful smile on her face as her hands are freed. She brings them to Priscilla's waist, guiding her to her side.

They lay, with lazy kisses and lazy hands on a lazy Friday night. A breeze hits them from the open window and the cicadas and crickets sing.

They want for nothing else.

# Chapter 13

dream.

Everywhere she looks, there are people —but not just any people, *her* people. Families, couples, children, elders, of all walks of life and diverging ascendancy yet so interconnected all the same — human, kelpie, orc, redcap, brownie, werewolf, witch, even her good friend Nessie had decided to so generously grace this afternoon with their presence.

All mingling, chatting, partaking in very fancy bread and wine, surrounding the birch tree, surrounding *Ainsley* with so much love. She had greeted every single soul that walked through her threshold today with the most heartfelt of smiles, and it is still not enough — she is theirs as they are hers.

Her eyes begin to water looking at it all, basking in the feeling and committing it to history, her history. Nothing can ruin this night — not even an old fool's fear of the wheel of time.

Today, she lives.

"I told you it was a good idea, didn't I, darling?" Estelle walks up to Ainsley, offering a listening ear. Her dark hair is tied behind her head in a fancy updo and her arm preoccupied with a glass of fragrant wine.

"Oh, Estelle, my good friend — never let me doubt you ever again." Ainsley locks her in a tight hug. "Words cannot express my gratitude. This would not have been possible without you."

"Oh, don't get all sappy on me now! Leave that for the end of the party, when we're both a tad more drunk." Yet she hugs Ainsley just as tightly.

"Then it is a promise — we shall fully reminisce later. But for now? Go! Mingle!" Ainsley ushers Estelle onto the mass of familiar faces — she might be the one organising this event, but while it happens, she is also a guest, and Ainsley will make sure she enjoys it as well.

So she does, finding her husband and children at one of the many tables, talking away with another acquainted family as she joins them.

It's a wonderful day, it truly is. But there is one final arrival Ainsley still expects to make it perfect.

Fashionably late, as it is.

Ainsley had thought the Priscilla she saw yesterday in that same pastel dress she wears now to be the pinnacle of beauty — a vision straight from her memories of the era of royalty, with all of the beauty and grace but none of the corruption of the soul.

But as she stands there, with Priscilla making her way through the wide open gates of her estate, Ainsley knows she is in the presence of true royalty — her Queen, the true vision of Paradise. She glows with a sun-lit halo, her face tinted by the subtlest rouge and glittery powder, the fabric of her dress bouncing with her excited hops as she approaches Ainsley, her hair partly tied back by a simple satin ribbon and adorned with rings of gold and showered by pearls.

Oh, what bliss, to be in the presence of beauty herself.

Her perfume is potent inebriation as she extends her hands for the taking and Ainsley pulls her into a gentle, simple, powerful kiss.

"Priscilla, my life, my everything — by all accounts, you look positively divine. I shall avert my eyes or be blinded by such warm radiance."

"Someone is in a very good mood." She giggles, still wrapped around Ainsley's neck and blushing at the barrage of compliments. "But look at yourself!"

Priscilla takes a step back, still holding Ainsley by her hand so she can take in the view.

Ainsley looks exquisite, exuding elegance in the way only she can pull off, by all accounts. Her dress is of simple design — a deep neck into a belt of the same material, cascading down to the ground and trailing behind her in a fountain of white, lighter-than-air muslin. Her arms now adorned with a dozen more bracelets and rings than usual, and her vines neatly gathered on the top of her head in a perfectly messy congregation of leaves — the bright green of them the perfect backdrop to a delicate arrangement of flowers in a crown.

She is all that is good and comforting on this Earth.

"There is one thing missing in your ensemble, however," Ainsley says in a performative, solemn voice.

"Oh? What is it?"

Ainsley brings her hands to Priscilla's head, hovering them over her, and she feels it again — that familiar energy surrounding them, making her baby hairs stand on edge. The warmth of it washes over her and in an instant, a garland of flowers magically sprouts over her head, falling silently around her in the same arrangement as Ainsley's. Primroses, hyacinths, baby's breath, lilies of the valley —

"Your crown, Your Majesty."

Oh, her crown. Priscilla does an exaggerated bow in curtsy with Ainsley following suit, a deep bow towards each other as they both struggle to hold giggles back.

As they are, despite their silly role-play, they truly look the part of the crowned Queens of May Day, in all their grace and wisdom — and ready to part with the bountiful Summer they bring amongst their subjects.

"Make way for the court of jesters, will ya?"

Orion interrupts their fantasy to announce the arrival of the rest of the Moores, all dressed to the nines, although in more modern fashions. Young Lucy hides behind her father's wheelchair as he makes his way up a ramp that appears magically — a spectral force that leaves speckles of light as he threads its length with another belly laugh to share.

"That's a neat party trick there, miss. This 'magic is real' thing won't get old too soon, I'll tell ya." He remarks, extending a hand to the host as he joins the conversation. "On behalf of all of us, lemme thank you again for your invite."

"In the eternity that I have been granted on this Earth, I have yet to find the magic we are allowed to be boring in any way, shape or form, Mr. Moore." Ainsley closes her hand around his, shaking it firmly. "Drinks and appetisers can be found along the left hall. Please, enjoy the evening."

"Ach, now we're talking."

Mr. Moore wastes no more time, making a beeline for the refreshments. Ainsley manages to catch his journey being interrupted by what seems to be an acquaintance of his, recognizing the man and giving him a shock as the unglamoured minotaur grabs his attention before he is missed in the crowd.

Ainsley almost expects the worst — a scene — and so early in the evening as well…

But as Mr. Moore takes some space back and squints, inquisition in his language at a stranger greets him, one that easily towers over his quite large figure. Mr. McDonald finally says the right thing, and Mr. Moore snaps his fingers and points at his friend, the pieces finally falling into place.

Their voices boom together in friendship and camaraderie then, appearances now being simply another layer to their relationship, but in no way an obstacle. Ainsley lets her anxieties go. She worries, she does, and she almost intervened to smooth things over, her body entirely turned to the event. It was not needed, evidently, and she is glad it is so.

Perhaps there is hope yet.

"Lucy, there's a playground in the backyard and plenty of other children to play with too." Priscilla sees the youngest of the Moores struggling in the crowd of adults, no matter how colourful and weirdly amazing they look. "What do you say?"

She nods enthusiastically, the promise of swings and see-saws bringing her to a full run as she dodges the crowd with Cass in tow.

Orion is the last to mingle — not out of anxiety or shyness, but because he had clocked that woman he had been in constant fights with, Amanda Nowak, as soon as he walked in. His enmity towards her is still clear, but Priscilla catches an edge of something else in his annoyed, audible 'tsk's he disperses in her direction, despite her being completely oblivious to them from this far. Something he perhaps isn't aware of yet himself, so she lets it slide as he excuses himself to grab a much-needed drink.

So, it is just them: Priscilla and Ainsley, hands together, looking out to a sea of faces — so familiar, yet so new at the same time.

Not for long.

"Are you ready, my Queen?" Ainsley breaks the comfortable silence between them to extend a hand in courtesy to Priscilla.

"What for?" A brow arched, yet she takes Ainsley's hand in trust.

"Your family is a delight to be around, and I am glad I had the pleasure of meeting them. Now —" Ainsley takes Priscilla's hand to rest on her arm as she leads her into the crowd. "It is your turn to meet mine."

And so she does, and what a delight it is too.

Of course, every family name she comes to know, every individual she meets for the first time, is an encounter to remember for the rest of her life on its own. The first hour of this party is filled with live music from a band playing on the second floor, good food, good drinks, laughter and handshakes with a couple of a dozen different hands — webbed, clawed, wrinkled, smooth, porous, of all sizes and ages. Those are easier for her to acquaint herself with — brand new faces she commits to memory, people who are clear pillars of this community much like her Ainsley is, be it for their skills, experience, or warm personalities.

It is harder to come to terms with those she had already met before, however briefly, she realizes. To rewrite her own perception of those she was already familiar with as she meets a much greener, much tuskier and somehow much bigger Mr. Hogg. The easiest is the Nowak family, as the only difference they pose is long insect wings on their backs, slightly pointier ears, and somewhat iridescent skin under the sun.

They find Amanda, the youngest, and Orion again — idly chatting away by the shade of a branch. They seem to have talked their conflict out, their animosity gone and a truce struck for the time being. Priscilla can't help noticing the way Orion looks at her, and she knows exactly what is going on inside his mind at this moment. His thoughts running wild and free — albeit in much more colourful words when it comes to him, she's sure.

It's hard, but not impossible. And as she meets more and more people and talks to them in earnest, coming to know them with interest, she finds their struggles painfully human — perhaps even more human than her own.

Potions and spells are not made to hex or poison, but to bring fortune so a child may pass their driving test successfully, or to give a friend a boost in confidence after a bad break-up. Natural powers are more often used to allow someone to work a side job to bring a nice gift to a loved one on their birthday than to scare some poor random trying to make their way home.

Their pains are so relatable — rent, work, school, and then the added complications of having to hide a part of themselves from the rest of the world. But so is their joy, unbridled as they are when they are free to come together to share their accomplishments with those who will understand.

Priscilla understands.

So, they eat, and drink, and talk, and *dance*.

Ainsley takes the first ribbon from the bunch neatly tied on her tree and brings it to Priscilla. She takes it in her hand, and this is no longer just a piece of satin she bought in the craft store and laboured to bring to this place, and then to tie them one by one on the Birch's branches for this exact occasion.

This is the first ribbon of a choreography she has no idea how to perform.

"Ainsley, are you sure —" She protests, trying to give the ribbon back to a much more seasoned dancer.

But Ainsley stops her, closing her own hand around Priscilla's on the string.

"You have battled more complex patterns before," Ainsley reassures her. "Fear not — a simple left and right around the person walking towards you shall do the trick. Take it slow, and feel the beat. Let your instincts guide you."

She brings their connected hands up and down as they sway in place together, mimicking the movement expected of her and as Priscilla nods in understanding. Ainsley hands half of the bundle to her so they might distribute it to the rest of the guests.

Priscilla, in turn, shares her half with Ian, who then shares it with his family. Ainsley takes her remaining stack and divides it again, passing it on to an excited Cass who remembers performing a maypole dance back in her kindergarten days, and shares her half with her family as they distribute them around the birch, and one by one the dance circles take place around the tree:

One on top as those with wings and brooms and other flight capabilities hover by the higher branches. One on land, as they take their positions facing each other for the dance. And a third one of scattered guests accommodated in their seats, ready to pass their ribbon to the next table.

Priscilla stands facing Ainsley, now calmer but concentrated, both of them with their respective strings in hand as the music begins.

All that Priscilla manages to do in the first few moments is to fail with grace, and so fail with grace she does. She stutters on her step and trips as she leaves Ainsley behind with every beat, trying to pick up her pace as she remembers her guidance. She almost overthinks it again, trying to visualise before doing and losing herself somewhere else, hoping she has enough tension on the string for her part in this weaving to count — but as her eyes land on a much clumsier Lucy as their paths cross in the main circle, her mind stills.

Lucy trips on pebbles, strays from her path, bumps into every person on her way around this circle — and yet, despite the 'sorry's she musters in between steps and giggles, her smile never leaves her face. Her ribbon, a bright green against the bark of the Birch stands out, contrasting in the criss-cross pattern being oven by the other dancers — sagging, missing spots, imperfect.

But Lucy doesn't care, and Priscilla doesn't either. For she dances, and so does Lucy, and Ainsley, and Orion, and Estelle, and so many others she has had the pleasure of meeting tonight. Each leaves their mark upon Ainsley's soul as best as they can, and that is enough — for they are there, and that's all that matters.

So back and forth Priscilla sways, twirling and laughing and greeting every face she comes across with a joy that spreads. She stutters no more, but that fact barely registers as she is taken by the music and the magic of the moment. Her path crosses Ainsley's now — Once, twice, three times as they get closer and closer to the tree and she feels the rhythm on her bones, the steps in sync and claps of those around them shaking the whole wide world.

Until it halts, music and all, and she is back where she began, facing Ainsley once more.

She looks at Ainsley, and Ainsley looks back, both of them breathless, both of them content, both of them *alive*. People cheer and celebrate, dispersing once more as they appreciate the Birch now completely entangled in the multicoloured ribbons.

Priscilla and Ainsley remain a while longer, just enough for Priscilla to throw herself into Ainsley's arms, dotting her face with kisses before they too look for a seat and drinks.

Something is wrong.

Ainsley thought it might have been her imagination trying to sabotage her on a perfect day like this, or perhaps just a trick of the alcohol already running full speed in her sap combining with the relentless heat of this afternoon in a deadly cocktail — but no. There is this clear, indescribable feeling at the pit of her stomach that has made itself known in the past half hour, but that she was only able to place now, as she sits alone on one of the scattered benches alongside the flowering railings that separate corridors and patio.

Magic has given her many gifts, and many curses as well. This is one of them — one Estelle is much more skilled at than her with her cards and tomes describing their visions, but Ainsley can access such knowledge on a much more instinctual level alone.

She remembers not when specifically she last felt this, but she remembers what accompanied it — the hurt, the pain, the betrayal at times. All is well now, her guests well taken care of as she's finally given a moment of silent contemplation, only to come to the realisation this night might be cut short not too far into the future.

She is not sure she is ready to face that reality yet.

Her only respite is seeing Priscilla again, two cups in hand as she does her best at politely dodging more conversation with the other guests, gaze darting around until finally finding Ainsley.

"There you are!" She hands one cup to Ainsley, sitting by her side and raising hers for a quick toast. "I thought we might need a break from all the drinks so I brought us some juice instead."

"And it is thoroughly appreciated, my sunshine. Thank you."

Ainsley chooses not to alarm Priscilla with something as vague as a bad feeling, deciding on instead sipping on the cold drink in comfortable silence as they watch the crowd from a distance, side by side.

It helps — the juice, bringing soothing refreshment for a little while. At least until Estelle approaches her with the last task of the night, before those with younger children need to part for bedtime.

"This is your speech, your party, Ainsley, I wouldn't want to —" Priscilla tries to explain as Ainsley brings her up the stairs to the upper floor, a small magical device much like a microphone awaiting her words as the string quartet makes space for them.

"Please?" It's all Ainsley can say to plead, a hand squeezing Priscilla's as they await Estelle's cue.

It's small, a crack in Ainsley's perfect image, but it's all Priscilla needs to understand something is afoot. So, with a small nod, she complies.

Ainsley turns to the crowd, any fleeting ghost of a worrisome look long gone from her face, a perfect mask cast. Priscilla follows closely, staying at Ainsley's side as she moves to address them all.

"I shall keep this short and sweet, for both your sake and mine." Ainsley begins, head held high, projecting her voice for all to hear. "Thank you for coming tonight and for partaking with me in this celebration of life. May Day has always been about rebirth, a tribute to the coming of brighter days, and I want to echo this message tonight. No matter what problems we might have yet to face this year, I know it shall be all right — for after a long winter, there shall *always* be spring awaiting us."

Ainsley catches Priscilla's gaze for a second with a smile and she raises her cup high. Below, every guest mimics her, raising their drinks above their heads as Ainsley readies to call for a cheer.

But she is unable to let the words out.

Something catches in her throat. It starts as a simple cough, a stutter that she brushes off, a hand on her chest as she tries to recover.

She is not afforded the respite, however, as another wave catches her. She grips the railing, trying to find balance and air. But if not for Priscilla coming to her aid and holding her by her waist, she would have met the same fate as the glass she had been holding onto earlier — splattered on the ground of the first floor.

"Ainsley! What's wrong!?" Priscilla cries out for her, but it is all a haze as she gasps for air.

She blinks hard to cast away the tears forming in her vision, and as she opens them again, she sees a faint cloud of dark smoke exit her lungs. Her hands are covered in fine soot, coarse as they blend with her bark skin and taste of —

"Fire."

# Chapter 14

"Ugh, lousy little —"

Mrs. Blair Ingram threads her way around the forest with much difficulty. No longer sporting her work uniform, her casual clothes still leave much to desire when it comes to comfortability, especially when traversing these woods.

It's not just that — it's almost as if this place is actively making her life harder as she tries to delve deeper. The trees, the bushes, the flowers, all conspiring against her to move a single inch over her path as she passed them by to make her trip, swerve, or otherwise be swatted on the face by a dry, hard branch that wasn't there two seconds ago.

How utterly demeaning. She is a respectable woman with a highly coveted job and, most importantly, an incredibly powerful spellcaster. A witch of her calibre should never even be considered for such a petty assignment in the first place.

Yet, here she is, on what was supposed to be her weekend off — hard at work for Gray Granite. Oh, joy.

The overtime pay almost isn't worth it.

Her phone rings, and she picks it up instantly.

"Is it done?"

"No, but I'm on my way. This place must be warded somehow, it's impossible to get around. She must know I'm here." Mrs. Ingram answers.

"Just make sure you're not caught. It's the entire reason we sent you in the first place, anyway — you're the only person in the area skilled enough to weave your way around any obstacles invisibly. Just leave the message and bail, you understand?"

"What do you even want me to write?" Mrs. Ingram asks. "I fail to see the point of a *message*."

"Anything vague enough not to be traced back, but threatening enough to keep them on their toes. It's not a mathematical puzzle, we just need them to know that it's in their best interests to cooperate with our vision peacefully, *or else* — etcetera, et. al., yadda yadda. You can be creative with the details."

Mrs. Ingram sighs, not even bothering to put the phone down as she comes across an open spot on a slope, perfect for their plans.

She gives it little thought as she lifts her free hand over her head, inscribing a sigil in the air. She needs no more — a simple fire spell to stamp the words onto the plant life laying there. It all looks so sad and devoid of life, too — between the threat and the trespassing, she is sure Ms. Wood will barely miss the lost flora.

But a vision interrupts her before she finishes her incantation.

Young, inexperienced, *weak* witches get unplanned divination visions — and Mrs. Ingram is none of those things. These woods must still be playing with her, somehow. She tries to fight it, but slivers of images hit her nonetheless.

The mansion she had been to mere days ago, full to the brim with magical and human folk alike.

Drinks. Food. Laughter. Music.

Ainsley Wood and Priscilla Cardoso, dancing around the tree.

A party.

Blair hesitates.

"Are you sure this is absolutely necessary?" She asks, but she gets a sigh back.

"You're asking the wrong person. Do it, don't do it, just tell me so I can write this report to our boss and be done with it."

Mrs. Ingram cannot fail, not now. She has been working on this promotion for too long for a stupid message to get on her way and taint her pristine record. It's them, or her.

So, she makes a choice.

"…It's done." She hangs up.

Quick. Painless. A cauterised wound — or so she believes. She lifts her arms again, picturing the message, weaving the incantation with her mind's eye.

She expects the words to materialise over the grass and other small plants of this meadow and instantly snuff, leaving only the charred remains behind in a neat font.

But how wrong she is — it's fast, *too* fast. The flames only grow from there, spreading to the rest of this area at a rate she has never seen before.

"Well, fuck—" Is all she can say. She tries to stomp on the flames to snuff them out, but between her useless shoes and her confusion, the fire spreads faster than she can keep up with.

It starts climbing on the surrounding trees, and before she can even think about conjuring some sort of spell to stop it from spreading any further, a gust of wind hits the entire meadow.

The fire rises. It hits her arms first, as she lifts them, and then the side of her face.

She screams in pain.

Her glasses fall on the ground and burn completely, melting into the earth as she runs away.

⚜

"There is a fire. In — in the forest."

It is all Ainsley manages to say in-between more coughs, her voice raspy in a whisper.

"A fire?" Priscilla asks, but not to Ainsley.

It reaches Estelle first, and then the crowd who takes it in silent understanding and implied worry. From her side vision, Ainsley sees a couple of those who can take flight do so, skirting in between her Birch's branches to scout for it. Anxiety travels in the whispers of the remaining guests.

It might have taken a second, or a minute, or an entire hour — Ainsley does not know. But Helen is the one to report back.

"Southwest, a couple of miles down the mountain. And the way the wind goes, it won't stop there. There's no sugar-coating it — it's bad, my friend."

But Ainsley doesn't need Helen to tell her that. She feels it in her soul, every inch of her insides alight with pain. This isn't the first wildfire to desolate parts of her forest, but it has never taken such a toll on her like it does now. Before, she would have shouted, rallied, ran to placate the flames however she could. But now? Ainsley would be lucky to get a few sentences out as she claws at her throat for purchase, in complete vain.

She looks around from her curled position on the floor, to her dear friends who look up to her so. Waiting for her to break the air of tension that has covered this party.

Ainsley readies to muster every single string of power left in her body so she can stand again, holding back every cough behind her throat and every tear that threatens to fall, to be the leader they so desperately need at this moment.

But a careful hand reaches her back, so soft, so caring. She looks to her side, to Priscilla — her face twisted in worry and momentary confusion. Yet she brushes Ainsley's vines from her face and gives her space, all while comforting her with words Ainsley hadn't heard in a long time.

"There, let it all out, Ainsley. We're here for you. We'll get the fire put out." Priscilla says with such conviction, Ainsley's resolve crumbles right there, right now.

For she is her Queen and this, too, is her queendom to protect.

It's clear as day to Ainsley, and she finally lets the soot and ash take over her body, the tears flow, her breath to be attacked, however painful it is to do so — she knows it will not be forever. Ainsley can scarcely hear it, in-between the coughs she splutters with new strength, but Priscilla exchanges firm words with Estelle, crafting a hasty plan of action in tandem.

She misses most of the details, but through her blurred vision, she sees her guests, her dearest of friends, move in groups. Parents take their children through the front door, to keep them safe and as far away from further tragedy — as they should. The remaining scatter out the back, skirts and sleeves pulled out of the way as they delve deep into the forest. Light spells and nocturnal beings guiding them, witches and fae scouting ahead through the small of a long night.

Ainsley fights every instinct in her to follow them as she is left alone with Priscilla. She should be there, with them, her people. These are her woods, her world, her everything. She knows it as well as the back of her hand because it is her, and she is it, as the flames inflicting her both outside and inside threaten to consume it all.

Through her turmoil, all she can do is hold fast onto Priscilla — who, despite being currently preoccupied with contacting triple nine, never lets go of Ainsley, her free hand steadfast around Ainsley's back.

"Ainsley, my Ainsley, my love, everything will be alright. It will be alright, I promise you. I promise." Priscilla says in a constant, reassuring whisper to her, as she continues to expel the cursed black dust from her mouth and it powders their skirts and the floor under them.

Ainsley hopes she is right.

❦

"It will be alright. Everything will be alright, my love."

Priscilla repeats it in a mantra, for both Ainsley's sake and hers. Estelle promised she would handle things to get this fire controlled, but if she's being honest — if she weren't here, clutching Ainsley as she struggles with every breath, offering her as much comfort as she can at this moment — she would be out there with the others.

What would she even do against the blazing flames? She has no idea. She's just human, after all.

But who can stand idly and watch the love of their life suffer like this?

"I — Priscilla —" Ainsley tries to speak in between her fits of coughing.

It has been an hour or so now. Priscilla did not dare move them from their spot on the second floor, so worried she was of injuring Ainsley more. Her mind has gone through every solution one would think of to help with Ainsley's coughs in her despair, but the logical part of her brain has kept her put by Ainsley's side. This isn't some common cold.

Ainsley is *burning,* only the flames are nowhere near her body, *this* body. Nothing Priscilla can do now will solve anything — all she can do is be there for Ainsley, to make her as comfortable as she can.

"Shh, don't speak, Ainsley. Please. Rest." Priscilla tries, but Ainsley struggles against her arms as if to break free.

One hour like this, coughing and struggling with every single breath. Priscilla had hoped that, by now, Ainsley would be showing some signs of improvement, any sign at all. But, if anything, her condition has turned so much worse. The soot now covers most of both their dresses. Her hands. Her eyes are dry, all tears spent as she struggles to open them.

"They need me — They — I can feel it —"

"Ainsley, you can't, you'll only hurt yourself more —"

It's in vain. Priscilla feels that all too familiar energy in the air, that build-up being sapped from the Birch directly into Ainsley's veins. It's magic, after all, and in an instant, Ainsley gains an amount of strength Priscilla has never seen Ainsley bolster before. She jumps to her feet and throws herself over the railing of the second floor, a vine catching her just in time by the waist before she flails and lands on the flowery, empty ground below.

"Ainsley!" Priscilla cries out, but Ainsley runs ahead and dares not look back, lest she change her mind.

Priscilla follows her outside, making the long way down the stairs and around the tables — and across the Birch. Vibrant with life just a while ago, now clear scorch marks burn through the tapestry of ribbons they had worked so hard to weave, cutting across them as they disintegrate into ash.

She won't allow the same destiny to reach her Ainsley.

"Ainsley, please! What are you doing!?"

But she is too late. With the magical burst of energy, Ainsley stands a good thirty feet away from Priscilla at the edge of the woods behind the mansion, and Priscilla has to shout so her voice can reach her.

Ainsley unceremoniously undresses, leaving her stained clothes there on the ground as she looks back to Priscilla one last time with her dry, empty eyes before leaving her behind for good.

"Stay. I love you, Priscilla."

A soft smile behind smudged soot and an empty promise. Just like that, she is gone into the night.

"Ainsley!"

No. Not like this.

Priscilla expects to lose complete sight of Ainsley then, in the low twilight — and for a moment she does. But as she ties her long dress up and around her waist, a figure emerges from over the trees in her view. Barely visible against the faint remnants of sunlight and the smoke that colours the night red, the silhouette grows in size with every step it takes away from Priscilla.

It's gigantic, monstrous, towering over the ancient treeline and walking around them as if it was a simple shortcut through a field of wheat. Its long talon-like hands brush branches out of its way — as if needed. It is as if the trees themselves move out of its path in a silent command, every leap of a step it takes shaking the ground below Priscilla and throwing her off balance, but other than that? The figure leaves no trace of its presence behind, every piece of the forest intact in its wake. A crown of sharp branches and thorns decorates and meshes into something that passes for a face — smooth, speckled bark — and those deep, muted black eyes.

"Ainsley…"

Priscilla says, but it is barely a whisper. Of course, she knows that Ainsley is this immortal, incredibly powerful spirit — but seeing it, right in front of her eyes as she changes and morphs into a creature not even her wildest dreams could conceive… It highlights the stark difference in their natures in a way Priscilla had not thought of before.

It's not a thought she has the time to entertain just now. She resumes her pursuit, ready to follow Ainsley into the dark forest, but the sound of an engine approaches her with speed. She whips her head back to be welcomed by a familiar sight — Cass's motorcycle, but it's not Cass who rides it.

"Holy shit! Is that your girlfriend!?" Orion stops right next to Priscilla to bring his visor up in shock, or awe — honestly, Priscilla cannot tell which.

"What are you doing here?" She asks. Priscilla distinctly remembers Orion and his family leaving with the rest of the guests to go home.

Priscilla wants to bully him back to town, but his expression turns grim.

"Fuck, you didn't hear?"

"Hear what?"

"The fire spread. A lot. Firefighters got my whole neighbourhood closed off, so I dropped everyone else at yours."

Realisation dawns on Priscilla.

"Orion, your home…?"

He shrugs it off, but to Priscilla who has been by his side for this long, he can't hide his pain.

"No idea, but it doesn't sound good. I got tired of sitting on my arse though, so. Here we are."

There is a moment of silence where neither wants to, yet they grieve anyway.

"I'm so sorry."

"Don't. Or at least not until we're done pulling our weight." He offers her a pathetic smile. "You're running after her, right?"

"Do you even have to ask?" She offers another one back.

Orion gives Priscilla an extra helmet and throws his head to the side.

"Hop on."

Orion has never been the best driver, and Priscilla knows this. She has always been grateful for him giving her rides everywhere, but the fact is that, if not for her being there to keep an extra set of eyes on the road, she could definitely see them being involved in way more accidents.

This isn't that. When you are riding on the back of a motorcycle at full speed, skirting around trees and jumping over bushes in the dead of night with only a headlight and your giant girlfriend to guide you? Any move that doesn't result in both of them crashing is good driving.

So Priscilla holds onto Orion for her dear life and they tail Ainsley as best as they can from afar.

It's a long, gruesome journey to the heart of this catastrophe. The smell gets them first — the smoke pools over them and intoxicates the air with its stench. Minutes of agonising pain hit them both as they get a fraction of the taste of what Ainsley had been experiencing for the past hour, their lungs struggling even under the protective helmets. Priscilla's stomach turns in renewed empathy,

Ainsley's desperation now so vivid in her heart as it aches as well.

Then, the gaping hole they find in the forest. Miles and miles of nothing more than charcoal covering what once was vibrant, alive. Priscilla wants to mourn it there, now, certain that she has been to this side of the woods before — on that fateful evening when Ainsley had taken her on that hike. She does not let herself linger. Not yet.

In the distance, they finally see it.

Fire. So much fire.

A wall of it, so bright, so loud, so so *warm*, even from here. Against the assault of her senses, she can see faint silhouettes battle it tirelessly. Estelle and the others have not given up yet, and that gives her small, but much-needed hope at this moment. With the faint call of sirens in the background, she knows there are people on the other side of that wall doing their best to placate the flames as well.

Priscilla wonders if they can even make it there, the thick remnants of the trees that once stood here blanketing the ground, blocking their attempts at delving any further. Orion has to slow down or be completely buried with it, but neither of them gives up yet — not when they are this close.

"Shit—" Priscilla curses under her breath. Not too far from them, Ainsley emerges from the trees as well. Priscilla can see her locking eyes with the wall of fire, much like she had done only a moment ago, and her heart breaks even further.

Ainsley wails, a guttural sound that resonates in Priscilla's chest and stabs it even further. She had already suffered so much, gone through so much tonight, but the visual confirmation suddenly turns it much more real than it has a right to be.

So she runs to it, her deep, otherworldly scream shaking the entire city as this force of nature loses control of instinct.

"Pri, focus! Hold on tight!" Orion shouts behind his helmet, making a sharp turn with the motorcycle.

Ainsley's desperation as she ran had shifted the debris just enough for a slightly easier path from them to thread. It's awful, and nauseating as they twist, turn, jump. But Priscilla can see the flames get closer and closer, and Ainsley gets further and further away from them.

"Ainsley!" Priscilla shouts from behind her, but between the engine, the fire, and her rage, it all falls on deaf ears.

Ainsley dives into the burning hell, hands first. With the desperation of someone who is currently on fire, she swings her arms deliberately, a sharp scream of pain each time she does. It's effective — with each swing more of the blazing forest is pulverised, dissipating into cinders in the air as she uses her own body to stifle the flames.

Fast. Precise. Agonising to see. A painful dance as she puts it out by the dozen feet.

Priscilla wants to avert her gaze, look away until this is all over and nothing about another thing to work through in therapy. But she can't. Ainsley is sacrificing so much right now — the least Priscilla can do is commit her heroism to memory.

"Estelle!" Priscilla calls out as the path of all involved in this mission converges. Orion stops the motorcycle a few feet away from Estelle and the two dozen odd magical beings currently interlocked in chants.

In any other situation, the current sight would be beautiful. A chain of people, hand in hand in a trance Priscilla can only assume is the deepest, most ancient of magic.

And she would be right. At the centre of this Estelle is the only one to have her hands extended into the air. Pure energy towers over her as she levitates in place, all of it converging high above the treeline currently alight as tempestuous clouds the size of a football field rain over them. Powerful, plentiful, ancient weather magic. Step by step, they make their progress as the water quenches the flames and gets absorbed into the crackly dirt.

"You have to move the storm, Estelle! Please!" Priscilla pleads to Estelle as Orion and she makes the last few metres on foot, struggling to step over the cinders as motorcycle and helmets alike are ditched behind them.

Estelle looks over her shoulder, doing her best not to break her concentration on this spell before addressing her in shock.

"Priscilla! Orion! What the hell are you doing here? I thought —"

"There's no time. Ainsley is trying to put out the fire right now! She's burning herself! You have to help her!" Priscilla pleads once more, pointing to her girlfriend currently knee-deep into the wildfire just a couple hundred metres away.

"That's Ainsley!?" The complete shock not only Estelle, but all the other people display at the revelation does nothing to calm Priscilla down. "Oh, for all the Gods left on this forsaken Earth."

Estelle curses under her breath as she tries to do way too many things at the same time — the spell, the conversation, her tumultuous emotions at her friend's predicament. It all weighs on her shoulders as they slump, her already sharp brows furrowed even deeper.

"We're already spread thin as it is, darling. If I try to steer us, the spell might just break before you can even see it." Priscilla can see her decision hurts Estelle more than it hurts her.

"Please," Priscilla begs one more time, her voice cracking with desperation.

Her clamour catches the attention of the others as they join in, encouraging Estelle in their own ways to take this risk.

"You can do it, Estelle."

"She needs us. C'mon."

"We have enough to do it. The last push is all we need."

"Fine!" Estelle erupts. "But we need the extra power. Get in here, you two."

Estelle commands them, but Priscilla and Orion look briefly at each other and back at her, confused.

"You think just because you're human you don't have any magic? Hah! Think again, my dear!"

They don't need a second sign to jump to action. With a nod, Priscilla and Orion extend a hand each, placing them on Estelle's back as they become part of this link.

It's the weirdest sensation Priscilla has ever experienced in her life — like dropping head first into a lucid dream you weren't given the keys to. All of her senses are attuned to every atom that composes her existence as her soul gets projected out of her body, fuelled into Estelle's own, and then onto the sky. In a perfect circle, those atoms rain back onto her skin, drenching her body and constituting her once more. Rinse. Repeat.

Yet, somehow, it is all so strangely familiar as well. This space she has been thrust upon, brimming with abundant energy just waiting for a command to be shaped into something else almost feels like…

Like *home*.

Suddenly, she is no longer just the Priscilla who stands at this interconnected line of people. Suddenly, she *is* every person in this line. She is their thoughts, their feelings. She is every droplet of water that falls from the skies and rejoins the ground to evaporate and start the cycle anew, and with every blink of her eyes, it all melts together even further. In that instant, Priscilla isn't just magical too — she *is* the magic. She sees it all in her mind's eye as she shapes it into what she desires with the mastery of someone who has been doing this her entire life.

The key has been with her all along.

She focuses on this feeling, grounding herself in it, letting it flow through her instead of against her.

She pictures herself by Ainsley's side — towering height and all. Taking Ainsley's burnt hands into hers, placing them ever so softly over her own heart as her tears fall onto them — a constant rejuvenating stream that cleanses any ailment away. Over, and over and over again until she is safe and sound, healed, nestled in Priscilla's arms.

So it is — and, for once, it's beautiful.

"What is going on back there!?" Estelle is the first to notice.

Where before they were gaining ground at a snail's pace, guided by Estelle — now, they glide. Their speed picks up as they carefully pivot their direction for their path to converge with Ainsley's in a burst of energy.

"Holy shit — Pri! You have wings!" Orion shouts, looking at his friend as he shields his eyes with an incredulous smile.

"What!?"

It's true. Bright, translucent, long feathered wings made of the same energy that is currently conjuring this storm flap behind Priscilla — not enough to make her fly, but just the right amount to give this entire endeavour just the push they needed, quite literally.

Estelle crackles loudly. "However you're doing this, darling, keep it up! We'll be there in no time!"

In this state, Priscilla cannot tell for sure how long it actually takes. She keeps her mind focused on this one picture, letting herself be lost in it just enough to bring fantasy into reality. Step by step, inch by inch as her wings work overtime, they swerve, they change — they are right there.

They encase Ainsley, bringing the storm right over her.

As the first droplets of water fall on her burnt hands and evaporate instantly, this giant, alien version of Ainsley stops. She looks up at the glowing clouds just above her head and recognises that familiar hum of her friends' magic, encasing her like a soft blanket as the rain pours on and on, stronger and stronger, washing away the ash. It covers her tired, spent body in relief as she slowly looks back, meeting the eyes of people she holds so close to her heart, right behind her, hand in hand.

Estelle, Edmund, William, Helen, even young Amanda, right next to Orion — and so many others she cares for.

And, of course, Priscilla. Her sweet, perfect Priscilla, the glow of this magic that emanates *from* her in the form of wings is nothing like anything Ainsley has seen before, her eyes looking at this unfamiliar face she bears with the same love she affords her more human visage.

It all overwhelms Ainsley — rage mixing with passion. Protectiveness. She lets the rain do its job, renew her with strength, and she runs into the wall of fire with open arms as she tapers the flames once more with her already stiff, broken limbs.

Together.

# Chapter 15

t's all a haze.

Ainsley's eyes open with enormous difficulty. Through the lingering smoke and clouds, she sees the twinkling stars of this beautiful night, sparkling on as if nothing is wrong. As if her body isn't in agonising pain, as if her arms aren't unresponsive, as if a crater hasn't materialised in her soul. As if she isn't currently small again, laying down on the memory of what once was part of her forest, unconscious for Gods knows how long. And perhaps, to them, nothing *is* wrong. What do they care if the fire has been extinguished? Or whether her beloved ones have too been harmed by it or not?

But as her vision clears, so do her other senses, little by little — until she can feel the soft caress of Priscilla's hand against her face, under the crippling pain she has no energy to express. Her head lays on Priscilla's lap, and under the ever-present smell of ash and smoke, the faint note of her perfume keeps Ainsley from absolutely detaching again.

Oh, it is quiet. Too quiet. All life is gone from that place.

Then, her friends' voices. It takes her a moment to finally make either head or toe of what they so urgently discuss, their feelings still raw and on the surface as their shouting reverberates into the nothingness they currently stand in.

"There's no question! Those wee fuckin' bastards from Hilltop! Mark my words, they're trying to scare us out!"

"That makes no sense."

"I'm not saying it wasn't, but there's no way we can ever prove anything."

"Oh, just let me get my powers back. No one is hiding from me."

"So we're just going to let them start a wildfire and walk away, free of consequences?"

"What do you suggest we do? Storm their building and kill their board of CEOs?"

"Aye, that's exactly what I'm thinking."

"What a bright idea, why don't we go ahead and dethrone the King as well?"

Ainsley understands no more as the discussion turns too heated, voices mangled and fighting for attention.

"Stop." Ainsley tries. But their voices are too loud, and hers too small as she still struggles to speak.

"Ainsley..." Priscilla is the only one to hear it, her hands careful as they cradle Ainsley's head, her voice quivering with sadness.

"Listen to me, I beg you." She finally musters enough strength for her words to pierce through the fight. "It's not so simple."

Silence.

Ainsley tries once more to stand up, to no avail — she's depleted all of her energy, magical or otherwise. All she manages is tilting her head slightly to face her dear friends as they gather around her.

"You cannae be serious." William protests, the soot covering his face gathering at his frown. "Look at your state, mate. It must've been a battalion of witches to conjure up all this fire. It was Hilltop, plain and simple. We cannae let this go."

But Ainsley shakes her head as another fit of coughs attacks her, leaving only space for a grimace.

"I am not denying their involvement in this, my friend. It wouldn't be the first time someone has attempted such an act of malice to this forest, to me. But this? This is different. This was *fast*."

"Ainsley. What are you saying?" Ethan asks. Ainsley sees his concern, but above all else, she sees the tip of his left wing — torn, broken, and she grieves for him too.

She grieves for all of them as she takes a moment to count the damage. Each and every one of those souls bearing a scar, a bruise, charred skin and spilt blood in equal parts.

"Look around you. Search your mind for recollections of the past month. How the weather has been brutal, how the sun has never felt closer to us. How the storm you have all so miraculously conjured has been the first sight of rain we have had for so long. How the wind has not taken but a moment of rest these past few days. Do you remember, my friends? Because I do. There has not been a moment since I've awoken when I did not feel its toll."

Ainsley looks at them, their shock, their denial, their hopelessness as they come to the realisation this amount of destruction was aggravated by something completely out of their reach.

"A single spark is all it took. Once, it would have devastated, yes, but not to this scale. Once, I would have been in fighting condition from the get-go. Once, this could have been prevented. Once. Not anymore."

Now, they stand in its aftermath — victorious, yet feeling defeated. All the rising feelings, the rage, the calls to action — they dissolve, evaporate, finding no ground to stand on again. Silence befalls them once more as plans fall apart, and the future seems so much more uncertain. As they finally take a moment to realise that what just happened cannot be fixed by their hands. Not fully, not now — perhaps not ever.

Except one.

With one hand, Priscilla comforts Ainsley, a thumb caressing her cheek as she props Ainsley's head on her lap. With the other she wipes away her own tears, her stifled sniffles and the cracking charcoal around them the only noise populating this tragic night now.

She looks up, with a smile of all things, and looks at everyone. Her best friend, her co-worker, acquaintances she has met mere hours ago.

Ainsley, her Ainsley, laying on her with barely enough fight left in her to breathe.

She finds herself feeling exactly what the others do, because of course — she is only human. Yet, at the bottom of this well they find themselves into, desperate as they are — she feels a strange sense of deja vu.

It's impossible to see the war when a battle has just desolated your heart. This, she knows well. Too well.

"Don't —" She finally speaks, and their attention turns to her. "Please. Don't give up. Not yet."

She meets their gazes, and behind their confusion such sadness plagues every single one of them. Yet all Priscilla sees is the fire — the one that is no more, brought down by their efforts — and she smiles.

"We've all just been through hell — of course things don't look good. We're in no estate for more fighting, so it all feels impossible. But it's not. I promise you, it's not. So please," She sighs and looks down at Ainsley.

She looks back, barely awake, and the tears Priscilla had been holding back start flowing once more as Ainsley smiles too.

"I mean, damn, look at us — we put out a wildfire, using nothing but magic. Your magic. *Our* magic." She shakes her head in disbelief. "It's nothing for you, maybe, but I can tell you right now I never imagined myself having this much power to change anything around me, much less on this kind of scale. Never, in a million years. Orion knows."

"Don't tangle me into this, woman." He tries to play it cool, crossing his arms, but he too stands exhausted — his once pristine blazer now singed at the hems. The corner of his mouth rises.

Priscilla chuckles in between her crying.

"So go home. Patch your wounds. Spend time with your loved ones. Rest. But tomorrow, when you wake up and it all seems like a waste of time, please — remember that you've already changed so much. You've given me a gift I can't repay —"

Priscilla looks down again, to Ainsley, and her words have never been surer.

"You've saved the woman that I love. And for that? I'll be forever grateful."

She looks deep into Ainsley's eyes, and there, she finds it again — that glimmer of hope, even in the darkest moments. Priscilla wants to kiss her, show all her love, but she does not dare disturb the thin peace they have, in case the smallest shift hurts her even further.

She doesn't need to — Ainsley does it. Despite the pain, the loss. She brings her burnt, stiff hand up just enough for Priscilla to take it into hers.

Priscilla doesn't look up to gauge the reaction of her friends, but she can hear their renewed spirits in the way they pick themselves up to do just that — go home, rest, gather what is left of their anger so they can fight another day.

For what is this anger but the purest form of love?

Priscilla and Ainsley stand on the empty patio of the mansion.

Once filled with laughter, now only ghosts roam the empty tables and ten the half-finished drinks lying about. The glass Ainsley had dropped over the balcony earlier still lies there, shattered into a million pieces as it decorates the grassy, flowery bed, reflecting the moonlight.

Priscilla wants to take Ainsley upstairs, and draw a long bath for both of them so they may assess the damage more clearly — so Priscilla may decide on the right amount of anxiety to feel. But Ainsley stops her and requests that Priscilla take her to her Birch.

So she adjusts her grip on Ainsley as she props herself over her shoulder, and she silently complies.

Together, they face the tree — it's just as they left it, still clad in ribbons, and even more deeply scorched underneath. Patches of black that do not mix, some still alight with vestiges of open wounds, cover the tree from roots to branches.

Priscilla wonders how long those roots are, and how much of them has been destroyed tonight.

Too much. It's always too much.

Ainsley makes to stand on her own before approaching the tree, but as soon as she tries to let go of Priscilla, her knees falter still. Priscilla catches her before she falls, closing the gap between them for her.

Ainsley painstakingly brings one of her now paralysed hands to it, to rest over the hurt bark of what she calls her soul. Her hand touches it and it does not splay — a permanent claw, a solid thud that catches on a ridge and leaves charcoal lines behind.

Ainsley winces before taking a deep breath. Again, as she had done earlier, she focuses on her connection to the Birch — it takes longer now as the post-adrenaline crash settles into her system.

Priscilla notices her struggle and she raises a tentative hand of her own, touching Ainsley's on the tree with all the care in the world.

She tilts her head towards Ainsley's, and she takes a deep breath with her.

In. Out. In.

It's delicate this time, almost a sheer filter over her senses, embracing both of them like a long-lost memory of a summer they have not spent together yet. Slowly, they can feel its flow as the tip of their fingers merge with the tree in spirit. Ainsley's hand, splintered, stiff — now regains life under the thick layer of ashes covering it, as her fingers slowly give against the trunk. Priscilla does her best not to push, simply laying her own touch over Ainsley's hand and letting this power wash over her like a conduit.

Slowly, Ainsley's hand gives and gives, until her palm lays completely flat against her tree.

In. Out.

With this incantation, it is only a few moments more until her other hand is also regenerated. The superficial damage is still very much present as she lifts them in front of her eyes, but as she slowly moves her fingers in waves, testing their somewhat renewed mobility — she knows it's only a matter of time until those wounds turn into faded scars.

They stay there for a moment, interlocked once more as this wave of magic passes.

"I thought I'd lost you." It's barely a whisper as Priscilla says it, furrowing her brows against Ainsley's shoulder.

"You must understand — had I not left to help, the damage would have spread tenfold. Had *you* not helped as well, I do not know what my fate would have looked like now."

Ainsley brings one of her hands to Priscilla's face, lifting her head so they may look at each other's eyes — her own already filled with tears as she brings their foreheads together.

"So… Thank you, Priscilla."

But all Priscilla does is shake her head.

"Don't thank me — we both did what we had to do. I'm just glad we're both still here."

"So am I, my angel. So am I."

They embrace, then, under the watch of the Birch as the wind sweeps its branches.

Tomorrow, they will rebuild. Tomorrow, they will fight. Tomorrow, they will contend with the future.

Tonight, they have each other.

# Epilogue

"Winter is so lonely without you, Ainsley."

Priscilla sits facing her Birch, on a chair she had moved there at the first sign of a chill in the air last year, in preparation for this season. The snow now covers every inch of ground and roof of the mansion, and the cold winter air settles around her despite her best attempt at keeping warm with a blanket.

A hand-knit blanket, in a creamy yarn with braided fringes on either short side, made by Ainsley as a parting gift as sleep would encompass her days. It now sits around Priscilla's shoulders, and Ainsley's smell lingers on it still.

Priscilla saw it all — how Ainsley would feel the need to nap more often as the leaves of her tree would cover the ground under them, how by the last few days she could barely keep her eyes open throughout the day. So Priscilla would find her fast asleep, with her knitting needles in hand, halfway through a line of stitches.

She would laugh, then, and make sure Ainsley herself was keeping warm while she slept. But Priscilla knew her work on that blanket — in the few hours of daylight she was afforded to continue crafting it — was one of the few things keeping Ainsley from worrying about her future.

Priscilla would worry, too. Neither of them knew what would happen once sleep took Ainsley for good this time around. It could be just a couple of months, it could be a year, it could be —

Priscilla doesn't even dare go there — before Ainsley left, they had talked 'what ifs'. And, while Priscilla found it helpful to share their thoughts with each other, to air their grief, well… Any attempt at a 'solution' was ultimately pointless.

So they have made their peace — and a promise.

The fact is, when they decided to be together on that fateful summer evening, they knew what they were in for. And, in the end, Priscilla doesn't regret any of it for a second.

Being by Ainsley's side this part year has been the best months of her life.

The tragedy of the May Day wildfire has ignited a sense of justice amongst those who were affected by it, tightening their sense of community like never before. After the situation was contained and heads were cleared, this group of magical folk formed around Ainsley, out of necessity to prevent such a thing from ever happening again. While their main goal at the time was to rebuild what had been destroyed by that fire, they did not let matters fall from history's memory — they made sure to make quite a loud, disruptive statement about Hilltop and Gray Granite's plans to the local Council — and to anyone that would listen.

Unfortunately, most of it would fall on deaf ears when it came to any governing power — they couldn't care less. As they protested, shouted, sued — the lawsuit would be dragged, on and on. To tire them out, to make people forget, to keep everything under wraps as much as possible. It's still open, to this day, postponed indefinitely.

It didn't stop them.

What would be a delightful surprise is that their plight resonated with others. Locally, yes, but their story would be noticed by the media and go quite far online as well. Other groups affected by similar tragedies would reach out in one way or another, to offer their support and gratitude. Suddenly, they would find complete strangers freely giving their time and skills to help with the debris clean-up and reforestation efforts. People who had no relation, no idea who Ainsley was or how their positive impact on that forest was vital to Ainsley's life.

People who were hurt too. People who were just happy to help.

And, throughout it all, the empty rooms of the mansion would start to feel a bit less so.

The Moore household would be the first to move in, temporarily, out of necessity. Their neighbourhood would be closed off for a few days after the fire until the firefighters were sure it was all completely safe for those evacuated to come back and assess the damage.

Thankfully, their house was mostly spared from the destruction caused. But until then, Priscilla's flat would be too small to hold all of them comfortably, so Ainsley did not hesitate to offer the mansion's premises to her and her family for as long as they needed.

Even after such a tragedy, as they opened bedrooms left empty for decades, cleared the dust and made them home, there would be little time to be consumed by worry. Their few days there would be filled with busy work with the party clean up — but also big meals around a full table, calm evenings overlooking the sunset on the mansion's roof, comfortable nights in good company, talking until the small hours when sleep would call.

Ainsley recovered fast. Within a couple of days, most of the damage was but a distant memory materialised in the scars left behind as her arms would take a darker colour than before. She would take her daily walks as soon as she could, being even more thorough this time — many of the animals displaced needed care, a guiding hand. Ainsley worked hard to give them as much help as she could and allowed herself time to mourn for all the flora that could not have fled too.

Eventually, the Moores would leave to return home, but Priscilla decided to hang around for a while longer — just to keep an eye on Ainsley's condition, just in case.

In truth, in these few days she spent living with Ainsley she had a taste of what a day-to-day with her looks like — and, oh, how sweet it was.

Lazy mornings, waking up by Ainsley's side and staying there, half awake, half asleep until their stomachs would cry for food. Breakfast, lunch, and dinner as they would take turns cooking, teaching each other new recipes and sharing memories. Quiet afternoons where Ainsley would tend to her garden and, ever so slowly, Priscilla would start to understand it better, her infamous grey thumb of death losing its potency under Ainsley's guidance.

Even her dreaded work-from-home-answering-email days would be made a bit more bearable by Ainsley's side, as they would set a table and chairs under the Birch's shadow and sit together — Priscilla on her laptop, Ainsley with a good book. Silent hours gone by as they both focused on their respective tasks — until Ainsley would bring them tea and biscuits for a break, unprompted.

Evenings cuddling in the living room, watching their favourite soaps together on the sofa until their eyes would grow tired or their hands would find each other and not let go. Either way, they would end up in bed, tangled in each other and eager to do it all over again tomorrow.

It was in one of those evenings when Ainsley asked her to move in, permanently, as Priscilla complained about having to make an entire trip back to her apartment for some trivial thing she had forgotten to pack.

'Am I sure'? Ainsley looked deep into Priscilla's eyes. 'My angel, your presence here has enriched my life in a way no other being on this Earth has in a long, long time. That empty space in my bed had your shape, all along — I just did not know yet. My heart is already yours. All I ask now is the privilege to share the gift of time with you.'

She would give so much more. Freely. Fully.

Six months. Six full months with Ainsley, living together. Setting up an entire room as her private office. Bringing her own touch to Ainsley's bedroom — now *their* bedroom.

Unlocking the nursery once more, this time not to dig up old memories but to make new ones. Renovating it, bringing life back into it so Tommy, Lucy and Mae alike would be able to comfortably sleep on the occasion Ainsley and Priscilla would be asked to babysit. Their visits would bring so much joy to this place.

So would everyone else's. It was rare if they went a single week without entertaining one or more of their friends for a spot of tea, or dinner. Their May Day plans might have been cut short — but the spirit of the festival was kept alive with those visits, every single week of those six months with Ainsley.

Six wonderful months.

Full of life.

Full of joy.

Priscilla craves a lifetime more of them.

"Oh, Priscilla, dear." Estelle breaks her silent prayer with a comforting hand on her shoulder.

"Estelle." Priscilla wipes away a tear before it forms. "You're early."

"The kids couldn't wait," Ian answers, bringing another seat each so they may join Priscilla in her wait.

Tommy, as always, makes a beeline to the second floor, eager to play with the many toys they keep in the nursery for him. He brings out his favourite action figures and rejoins them to play pretend around the patio.

Mae, however, comes to Priscilla in her usual silence, side-eyeing her and expecting Priscilla to ask.

"Hi, Mae." Priscilla smiles. "How's the witchcraft lessons going?"

Mae shrugs, but the corner of their mouth rises. She takes one of her hands out of her pockets and takes her time inscribing a sigil onto the air with her index finger. A gust of wind bursts from it, tousling their hair even further.

"Whoa!" Priscilla claps at her fast progress. "That's incredible, Mae!"

"They're a fast learner," Ian adds, winking at Estelle. "Watch out, we might have a new head witch at the Lorelei-Waris coven soon.

"Oh, darling, Mae still has a lot to learn before the student surpasses the master." Estelle lovingly brushes away the hair from Mae's face, despite her grunts of annoyance. "But it's a promising start."

"Mae! Mae! Do it again!" Tommy pleads to his sibling, lifting his caped superhero action figure over his head.

Mae aims, reproducing the same incantation towards Tommy. Another gust of wind catches him, this time sending the toy flying in the air a good few feet before landing on the snowy ground.

"Yeah!" Tommy cheers, promptly turning into his wolf form to chase the toy as his family laughs.

"It's not that late to join Mae, darling." Estelle reiterates an offer she had already made Priscilla before, after her incredible display of magic on instinct alone.

"I'm sorry, Estelle." Priscilla had already politely declined in the past, and these few months she had spent with Ainsley had only solidified her stance on her witchcraft initiation. "I'm happy being the good old boring human of the family."

Her episodes had finally dwindled to a point where she would only experience them sporadically, and only for a few minutes at a time. She fears that, if she were to tap into her daydreaming (even consciously) it would simply set her progress back. It's just not a risk she wants to take — however enticing the promise of power is.

Estelle understands, but she laughs at that description.

"You're many things, darling, but boring is not on that list."

"Seconded. Not that she'll listen to me."

Orion breaks the conversation, making his entrance known with the rest of the Moores not too far behind.

"What are you weirdos doing outside in the cold? We can't have dinner here, the soup will turn into the world's biggest ice cube." He says, a container the size of his head in his hands.

"Orion!" Priscilla rises from her seat to give her best friend one of her signature tight hugs. "You made it!"

"Ugh, Pri!" He would tap her arm for release if it wasn't busy. "'Course I'm here. I wouldn't miss it, dumbass."

Orion's work has kept him incredibly busy these past few weeks, so for Priscilla to see him again in person is a nice surprise.

"Estelle, a hand?" Cass calls out from the front door. "The ramp seems to be blinking on and off again."

"Again?" Estelle sighs. "I need to do a full sweep, soon. I swear, if I didn't know any better, I'd say this place is haunted, darling."

Estelle stomps her way to the front doors to get it all sorted — for as long as that patching will last — and an excited Mae joins her to help.

It's impressive how easily they all settle into conversation. With the ramp fixed, one by one they join the circle that forms around the Birch, laughter and the noise of Lucy and Tommy's footsteps at play filling the halls of this slow Saturday afternoon.

'How's work?' 'Who's watching the finals?' 'Lucy's cold is completely gone, thank the Gods.'

It's simple, Priscilla knows. Once, it felt so alien to her. She wonders when exactly she lost that feeling; when she replaced it with the warmth that fills her heart now.

Eventually, the cold begins to creep over even the thickest coat among them. Those threads of conversation that tie them together around the Birch are thick and take them inside, slowly.

Priscilla is the only one to linger.

She stays there, her gifted blanket tight around her shoulders as the wind threatens to blow it away, her gaze locked on the Birch — on Ainsley.

Priscilla steps forward, closing the distance between them.

She's lovely. Even almost bare as the winter that has left it, branches splayed over the rooftop of the mansion and covered in white, sizeable bunches of young leaves ready to grow into spring as it announces itself.

This close, Priscilla can feel that familiar hum again, the magic inherent to this place so real as she places a soft touch on her.

Priscilla is silent, a prayer in its purest form as she lets her own breath align with the rhythm of Ainsley's song.

"Rest well. Take your time. We'll all be waiting for you, Ainsley — right here."

Another breeze embraces Priscilla, but she doesn't feel cold.

She's ready to join the others, then. Ready to let the course of time play its game as she makes her way to the kitchen, for another family gathering as they fight over what side dish will be the winner this week.

Ready for another year.

She hears the leaves first, rustling in the wind. Then, her first breath, an inhale almost lost in the cold air around them. Her feet land her on the ground, softly, imperceptible as her steps melt away the ice and in its place, snowdrops bloom.

Priscilla turns.

Naked, her vines billowing behind her in a cape of a green so bright, so full. The scars she bore from the fire are now completely gone. Her smile opens as their eyes meet, and a choir of birds sing her arrival for all to know.

"Ainsley!"

Priscilla cries out, and heads turn to witness. She runs — fast, throwing her arms over the love of her life and holding her tight, oh so tight, never letting go.

She's back.

"Priscilla." Ainsley holds her too, her first exhale uttered in her name.

They sway, spin, locked in place just taking each other's existence in as flowers bloom all around them. The others join with cheers and Priscilla transfers the blanket that had kept her company in Ainsley's absence onto her shoulders.

"I can't believe you're actually here. I've missed you so much." Priscilla shakes her head, the tears she had been fighting all day finally flowing.

"So have I, my angel. Unimaginably so." Ainsley caresses her hair. How it had grown too, her curls free around her perfect face.

"Not a day too early, not a day too late either. What did I say, darling?" Estelle throws a smug wink at Ainsley. "You just needed a nudge."

"Auntie, auntie! Can you play with us? Please?" Tommy calls, gently tugging on the blanket around Ainsley.

"Pretty please, auntie Ainsley? We want to swing again!" Lucy chimes in with an excited hop.

"Kids. Give the woman some space." Mr. Moore warns.

It's not just them — everyone else has missed Ainsley's presence in their own way — a listening ear, good advice, someone to gossip with, a fellow football fan. They each take their turn to impart a handshake, a hug, a kiss on the cheek to greet her once more and hope for her continued health. She takes them in kind, knowing she will be afforded another year of small delights like so.

But one of those delights she has been looking forward to all these wintery months. One she cannot wait for any more.

"While I would love to reminisce and catch up on all that I have missed while I slumbered—"

She turns back to Priscilla — her angel, her love, her May Day flower. Ainsley takes one of Priscilla's hands into her own, all eyes following her intently.

"I have a promise to keep."

She kneels.

"Ainsley…"

All she has in her person is the blanket that covers her, the feelings in her chest and the magic that permeates this moment.

It's all she needs. She takes Priscilla, bringing her for a brush of the lips, a chaste kiss over her hand. From the contact, flowers bloom — violets, forget-me-nots, lilies, baby's breath — wrapping stems and leaves in a ring around her finger. One that will live for as long as she does.

"Priscilla. Will you —"

"Yes!" Her tears have stopped, and all she can do now is smile from ear to ear, her cheeks alight with her racing heart. "I'll marry you, Ainsley, of course I will!"

It's all she needs to hear. Around them, their families cheer as Priscilla lifts Ainsley from the ground and kisses her.

Two souls, one dream, and the flowers that bloom for the life just ahead of them.

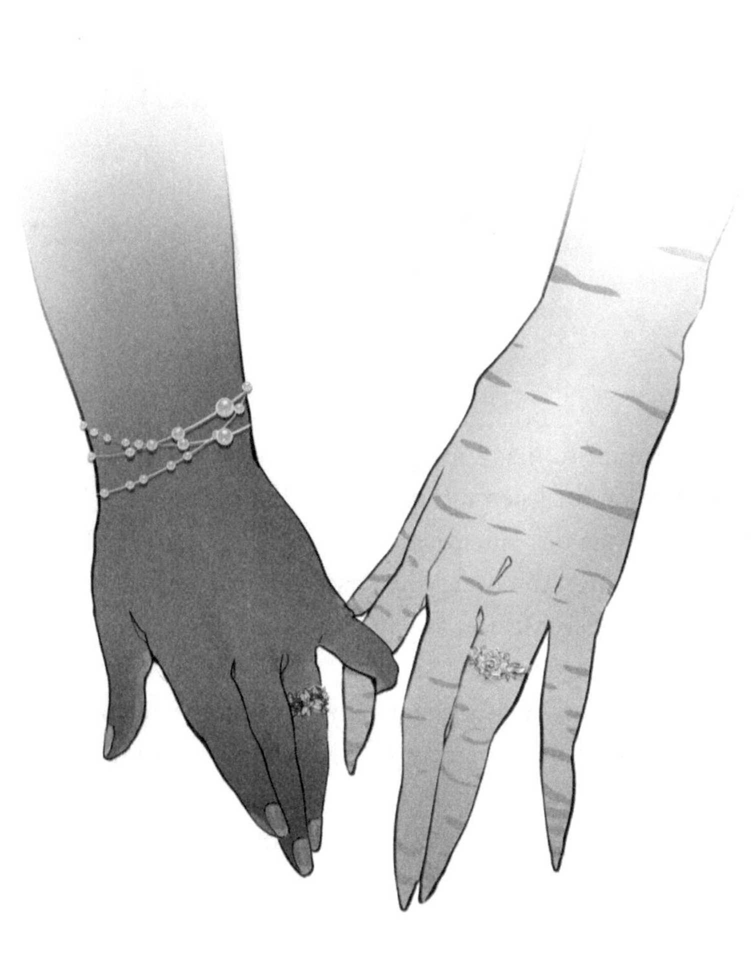

# Acknowledgement


I want to thank my partner in crime and in life, Top Hat Man, for listening to me info dump about this book for months on end, when it was still just an idea I was entertaining. You were the first and will always be the biggest believer in me, as you've told me yourself countless times. I love you~

I also want to thank my community who have gathered around my streams for hanging out (and thirsting over my characters) with me as I illustrated this book, and consequently the incredible alpha and beta readers I have found there:

Erin (HeyDinoKitty) for your incredible ability to see the big picture and support when I wanted to scrap the entire thing. You're one of the kindest souls I've ever met and your feedback tied this story together. GrayDollz for your sweet words and sharp eye for all those typos I missed (Gods, there were a lot). CrystalNova for your timely thoughts on the finished story before imposter syndrome took over and made me want to give up (again). The May Day Flowers ARC team for all the love and hype you've given to this book. And so many others who were willing to give my story a chance.

Without each and every single one of you, this book wouldn't have happened. I appreciate you so much.

And you, the one reading this book! Thank you for making space in your head for all these characters and this message I so needed to get out. I hope you found comfort in it as much as I did.

# About the Author

Sami (they/them), self proclaimed fae royalty and hopeless romantic, is a queer Brazilian artist now residing in Scotland. Having worked in 2D animation, dabbled and published in comics, now they find their first writing challenge by doing what they love most: making their OCs kiss.

faerisami.carrd.co
twitter.com/FaeriSami
twitch.tv/faerisami
tiktok.com/@faerisami
instagram.com/faerisami